DANCE OF FLAMES

ILIA CHRONICLES PART I

JORDANNA JADE

CHAPTER 1

A<small>IDAN SHOULDN'T HAVE BEEN ON PATROL ALONE, BUT WITH HIS PARTNER</small> attending to other business, he'd gone and taken their beat by himself.

The late sunset had the sky burnt orange as children played rough and tumble in the heat, their parents probably still on their way home from a hard day's work. It was one of those lazy kinds of evenings, where there was little to see and even less to do. In the city of Aquiline, the eastern most district of Ardr-end was not often the site of much discord. When it was, it was usually petty crimes, a young woman crying out for help after her bag had been ripped from her grasp, or a fistfight between men a fraction too drunk to function properly.

But despite its tendency towards peaceful nights, it was still Aidan's set route, so he walked it regardless. Though it was unfavourable for a man of his lower rank to patrol alone, Erica was tied up with her own situation, so there was nothing for it. Sometimes, his job required compromise.

For one night, he could handle a quiet stroll.

He was a sturdily built chap who wore the Ilpolitia's badge proudly on his standard-issue uniform, his name standing out in the embossed, golden lettering. More children zipped past him, giggling in their little groups, while sweaty men and women went on their way, bemoaning the heat. It was typical. Ordinary. Nothing he wouldn't see any other day.

He should have been grateful for it. In his line of work, a quiet night meant an easy night, but that also meant it was boring. Without Erica to keep him entertained with her brand of zany commentary, he quickly found his focus drifting, growing as muggy as the summer air. First, he thought about what he'd have for dinner. Then, he thought about finishing that poem for that girl he was sweet on, Leanne. Perhaps Erica would proofread it for him, but he only laughed at himself for the thought. No, it was much too embarrassing to show her.

Ahead of him, Mellingdale was coming up, a little neighbourhood that sent shivers down Aidan's spine despite the heat. He tended to rush through it when it came up on his beat, and for good reason; the place set his nerves alight. Six months prior, he and Erica had been on patrol there when a terrible fire broke out, tearing through the wintry weather like a demon. Thanks to their efforts, most of the civilians had escaped the carnage, but it had claimed the life of one man, the very person who had started it.

Justice, Aidan had called it, but it still felt like his spirit haunted the streets. The perpetrator had been an Ilia, one who could manipulate fire, and he'd lost his way like many of his kind did. People like him were the reason that Aidan had a job; the Ilpolitia dealt with crimes pertaining to the extraordinary, the kind of thing that the regular Politia were ill-equipped to handle. They kept the public safe, or, they tried to—but not everyone could be saved.

It was something that Aidan had difficulty coming to terms with, but it was the truth. The fire still haunted his memory, and he could still smell the smoke if he thought hard enough about it, acrid and eye-watering. But then he forced himself to put the memory aside, and it was then that he realised he could still smell it.

It didn't have the scent of some harmless kind of garden bonfire, either.

Looking around, he couldn't see any immediate cause for concern, but the very fact that the scent was there was reason enough to investigate further. He pushed himself onwards despite the dreaded neighbourhood's ugly appearance, bypassing the street that had originally burned in its entirety. There was still debris left behind there. Though the city's council had torn down the remnants of the ruined homes, the mess remained. It was likely that they didn't want to spend the money, not on Ardr-end, the second poorest district in the city.

Mellingdale was ghost-like, cool. It seemed as if the fast-approaching summer didn't actually reach the area. Aidan turned onto another street, still populated by residents, where the air grew hazier. Though most of Mellingdale had survived the fire of half a year ago, it had left its mark on the area. Many civilians had already come out of their homes, families milling about on the street as they, too, tried to figure out what was going on.

"Excuse me," called a young woman. "You, in the uniform, are you Ilpol?"

Aidan nodded, gesturing to the badge on his chest. "Is everything okay here?"

"Does it look okay?" asked an older man who stood beside her. He was half bent over, relying on a walking stick. "I've been calling on the bloody Ilpol for weeks, I have, telling them that that wild-fire Ilia has been running around here! You know what they said to me, boy?"

"No?"

"I knew it! Sodding Ilpol and their sodding cuts, they don't even inform their own. They told me that I was seeing things! That I should mind my own business because Ezra Purnell is dead!"

Ezra Purnell. Aidan felt that chill up his spine again. That name was familiar in print; it was the name of the Ilia who'd set Mellingdale alight, the name of the sole person who had lost their life in the blaze. "What do you mean he's been 'running around'?"

"It's true," the young woman said, nodding solemnly. "He's been here and there, asking about Dominique and Caspian, he lived with them when the fire broke out, you see. We went to the Ilpol, we all did, but they said there was nothing they could do. 'You're seeing things, he's dead,', that's what they kept saying."

Aidan wanted to deny it, but it sounded like the Ilpolitia. Stretched thin as they were, they hardly had the time to deal with every little concern. All their manpower went into detaining and stopping Ilia who were actively committing crimes, or others who were considered a danger. A dead man wouldn't be worth the time or money it would cost for an investigation.

"You think he's here then?" Aidan asked.

"Smells like he is," muttered the old man.

So much for a simple patrol. Aidan knew he could hardly just finish his beat and go home now. "I'm going to take a look. You all need to go home; this is in the Ilpolitia's hands now."

"Like that means much," someone else scoffed from behind him.

That stung a little, but he couldn't let it get to him. Keeping his head high, Aidan marched through Mellingdale, keeping his fingers crossed that the situation was more innocent than it seemed. It was unlikely. That old saying was rarely wrong; in his experience, when there was smoke, there was *always* fire.

The haze thickened by the second. Behind a set of bins, he found something that made him pause. A little flame, a wisp of a thing that didn't grow larger, nor did it catch onto any of the grim rubbish that hadn't quite made it into the bins themselves. It looked like a flower, ready to bloom at any moment.

He knelt, reaching towards it. It gave off a surprising amount of heat, but still, it didn't set anything around it alight. Wiping his forehead free of sweat, Aidan considered the situation. A controlled speck of a flame—that wasn't natural. There was no way that something like this wouldn't have set the bins up in flames, given the sheer number of greasy fish and chip wrappers that surrounded it.

That meant someone else was controlling it.

He tried to stamp it out, but the tiny flame was resilient, refusing to be felled. With no other way of putting it out, Aidan committed the area to memory and headed back out, searching elsewhere. Down back-alleys, behind homes, he found other, similar flames, each one in the same state, not quite alive, but not quite dormant either. There had to be someone around who he could pin the blame on, but the question was *where?*

It hit him as he was turning back onto the demolished street. There was one place he hadn't looked yet, and that was the site of the original fire. It had been a little house once, home to three. According to reports, people often complained to the regular Politia about the noise from that house, that sometimes they could hear a woman screaming or crying, that they could hear a man shouting, thumping, crashing around.

But, apparently, whenever they investigated, the woman always answered the door with a smile on her face.

Aidan hesitated as he came near to the ruined property, but he knew there was nothing else to be done except investigate. Steeling himself, he searched for the courage he knew he had, and made his way on down.

He realised quickly that he was not the only one there.

Midway down the street, a man stood in front of the home that the fire had started from. The debris before him was smouldering. The smoke's source? It wasn't quite a fully-fledged blaze yet, but if the man was the cause, then Aidan had a feeling that it wouldn't be long before it was. Though he wasn't armed with anything more than a baton, he had to act.

Going back to the Ilpol Offices to request back-up was out of the question. They were located back in Risthe-end, the opposite end of the city. If Aidan left to get help, by the time he returned, anything could have happened.

Slowly, he approached. "Excuse me, do you mind if I ask you some questions?"

The man didn't turn, but even from behind, Aidan could tell he was dangerous. His hair was shaven, probably in an attempt to hide the red that could still be seen clearly in the short strands, but more pressing was the bracelet around his wrist. It was coloured red, denoting him as a specific kind of Ilia. An Elementra, one who could control and make fire.

If the old man was right, then he was also the man who had been thought dead for the past six months.

"Excuse me," Aidan said again, raising his voice. "My name is Aidan Hopkins. I'm an officer for the Ilpolitia. Is that fire natural, or are you the cause?"

Still no response. The smouldering debris crackled. Aidan reached for his baton. "Sir, I need you to answer my question. Is that fire natural, or are you the cause?"

The man rolled his neck, and then his shoulders. When he finally turned, Aidan resisted the urge to bolt. Ilia who were addicted to their own magic were easy to spot, because the more they relied on their power, the more that power began to consume them. This one had nearly been swallowed whole, his eyes bright red, magic swirling about his pupils. His face was gaunt, and worse-still, entirely disfigured with mottled, twisted scarring. Much of his skin was the same, horrific burns, the sort that spoke of something that would have killed an ordinary man.

"You're all alone, Officer Hopkins," he said. "I thought Ilpol were meant to patrol in pairs."

The answers to Aidan's questions were in the man's appearance, but he'd always been taught to examine every possibility. Ignoring the comment, he asked once more, "Did you set this fire?"

The man cast his gaze back towards the burning debris, a smile cutting through his face. "I did."

"And the other, small fires I found? Were they you as well?"

"What do you think?"

"Do you have a license to practice magic?" Aidan asked, even though it ultimately didn't matter. Even if the man did, arson violated its terms.

Instead of answering, the Elementra only gave him a nasty look. "Why waste your time asking questions when we both know you already have the answers? Or is it my time you're trying to waste?"

Aidan finally took his baton in hand. "I don't make assumptions. I'm need to request that you come with me. What's your name, Elementra?"

The man's eyes flicked to the baton. "Officer, you're insulting me if you think that's going to be enough. I've got somewhere to be, so before things get ugly, I think it's my turn to ask you a question. Dominique Delacroix and Caspian Fay. You ever heard of them?"

The woman who answered the door with a smile plastered to her face. The man who shied away from any kind of questioning. They were a pair of Elementra Ilia who had escaped the blaze alongside the rest of the street, victims as much as anyone else, their names linked to Ezra Purnell.

"That's not relevant right now." Aidan stepped forward. "Sir, I'm placing you under arrest—"

The man moved, faster than Aidan expected. As a fist drove itself into his stomach, Aidan raised his arm to strike, but the blow caught him off guard. The force of it knocked him off balance, pushing the air from his lungs. As he staggered backwards, he forced himself to drag a breath in, striking with his baton once more.

The man sidestepped the clumsy blow, catching him by the back of his shirt. "Thought you patrolled in pairs to avoid getting beaten into the ground."

Aidan tore himself free of his grip, twisting so that the smouldering debris was behind him. He swung upwards, slamming the baton into the man's jaw. Inwardly, he congratulated himself on the well-placed strike.

But it wasn't enough.

The man hardly reacted, like he hadn't even felt it. If Erica had been with him, she could have backed him up, but he was all alone, facing off with an Elementra that had access to more power than Aidan could ever imagine. He was so far gone that physical blows seemingly had no effect on him, his magic having taken him over entirely.

Striking again, Aidan hoped to hit home, only for the man to bring up his arm to block it. His method wasn't working, but he had nothing to fall back on; there was no way to win fairly when he was so disadvantaged. The only option was to go all out.

"Back down, or I will need to use excessive force!" he cried.

The man's eyes flashed, and, as if it was reacting to his rage, the smouldering debris behind Aidan roared. It overpowered the natural heat of the evening; he could feel it searing against his back.

When he craned his head around to look, his breath left him. It was no ordinary fire, having grown immense in a matter of seconds. It could engulf the entirety of Mellingdale if this man wished for it. There was no way Aidan could turn tail and run now, but there was no time to gather his courage either. He could only act.

Rushing forward, he went for the man's knees, swinging the baton with all his might. Get him down and get behind him, if he could do that, he could gain the advantage. It would give him something to work with.

But the Elementra was just too fast.

He caught him, grabbing Aidan by the neck with fingers that were red-hot. Aidan dropped the baton with a cry, his skin burning beneath his touch. He clawed at the man's arm, trying to wrench himself free, nails digging into skin.

The other man's grip was absolute.

"Who are you?" Aidan gasped out, barely able to speak through the pain. The scent of burning flesh filled the air. Panic scratched at his insides.

"You know who I am, Officer," the man said, his voice curling around the words with a sick sense of delight. "Not very good at your job, are you? Thought you lot were trained better. I'll do the ol' Ilpol a favour then and take one off their payroll for them. Surely then they'll thank me."

Another laugh. Aidan realised what he was about to do, but it was too late. He thought of Erica, and how he never should have gone alone. He thought of the Ilpolitia, and how he'd let them down.

"Guess you're just fuel for the flame," the man said. "Thanks for the help."

A smirk. A roaring dissonance of flames. He threw Aidan backward, directly into the hungry mouth of the fire.

It swallowed him whole.

CHAPTER 2

Across the city in a bustling Caul-end pub, a woman sat at the counter and watched a matchstick burn.

Dominique held it delicately between her fingers, watching the flame as it danced. She regarded it as one would a lover, savouring the warmth and energy it gave off. It was the kind of thing she could stare at forever, whiling away her life in the light of the blaze. Beautiful. Powerful. Addictive.

She hadn't struck the match to light it, but had instead created the flame with her own hands. It was within her right as an Elementra because her magic was what made her, both in her blood and her soul. It whispered to her when everything else was silent, and it gave her the comfort she needed when the rest of the world got to be too much.

Tonight was an example. She'd come to the pub after hearing that it was the perfect place for people like her to spend time. So far, they hadn't been wrong. The Otherground, it was called, a place that was nestled in a nook of Aquiline's seedy northern district. Ilia swarmed all over it, people just like her having their fun.

"Hey!"

Dominique snapped her head up, making eye contact with the bartender who had called out to her. She found herself being glared at by a tall woman with warm, brown skin and voluminous, bouncy hair. A bronze stone hung from a chain around her neck, glinting in the light.

She didn't look like she belonged behind the counter of some dodgy bar, but there she was regardless. "You. Yeah, with the match. Put it out. Now."

Dominique hesitated. She wanted to keep it burning until the very last moment, to watch the final flickers of the flame, but she also didn't fancy being kicked out. Clasping her hand around the matchstick's head, she snuffed it out with a scowl. "Happy now?"

The bartender didn't look satisfied. "No. You here to sit and light matches with your fingers, or are you going to order something?"

With a sigh, Dominique tucked the burnt-up matchstick into her pocket. Her tricks would have to wait until later. "I thought this was supposed to be a safe space for people like me. You're saying I can't play a little?"

"That's exactly what I'm saying. You new here, firecracker?" The bartender paused, only to shake her head. "No, wait, stupid question. Look, The Otherground's no 'safe space' like you Ilia pretend it is. I turn a blind eye, sure, but that doesn't mean that the Ilpol don't stop by every now and then."

"That just means they don't come by all the time," Dominique pointed out.

"Just because it isn't raining all the time, it doesn't mean it won't. Ipso facto, don't do magic in my place. Now, you gonna order something, or are you just taking up a seat that someone else could use?"

Dominique wanted to argue, but the look on the bartender's face told her that there was no point. Her magic whispered in her ears, buzzing in her blood as it begged to be let free. *Burn this place to the ground,* it said. *Burn it down. Burn it down. Burn it down.*

That voice had been getting louder lately, harder to ignore. Forcing herself to focus, she turned her attention back to the bartender. "Fine, your choice then. Something strong, if you will. And cheap. Cheap is important."

The bartender nodded, turning away to make her a drink. Dominique fished out the money. When their hands brushed against one another, the bartender stilled—but Dominique only focused on the drink.

When she knocked it back, it burned its way down her throat. The alcohol made her wince. "Ah, thanks. What's your name?"

The bartender stared at her own hand instead of replying, a morose expression on her face. Dominique wondered if she'd accidentally burned her. "Hey. Hello? I was speaking to you."

Blinking, the bartender looked back up. "Sorry. It's Cami. Yours?"

"Dominique. Call me Domi. We sound kind of similar, huh?" Dominque put the glass down, running her finger around the rim. Anything to keep her mind off playing with fire. "So, tell me, Cami. Do you see a lot of Ilia around her?"

Cami looked at her, but her gaze was anything but ordinary. It felt like she was looking past her skin and into her veins, peeling her muscles away to see the bones beneath, peering into every little thing that made up who she was. Dominique wondered if that was the power that bartenders held, something they learned after spending forever listening to the woes of drunkards. Though she wasn't about to share all her dirty secrets, she couldn't deny that there was something enticing about the idea.

"I see plenty," Cami said eventually. She gestured to the bracelet Dominique wore around her right wrist. "Your kind are rarer around here, though. I know more than my fair share of bare-wrists."

"Not surprised. Being registered sucks." Dominique looked down at the bracelet now that attention had been drawn to it. Hers was red, marked with flames, telling the world that she could set it alight in a heartbeat.

"That's how it goes here in Aquiline. Can't say I agree with it all, but there are plenty of scum out there that make them think it's necessary, you know?" Cami let the question hang in the air a moment before continuing. "I see enough of those types come through here."

"Not everyone's using their gifts for good, or some crap like that?" Dominique laughed, tipping her glass towards Cami. She refilled it before handing it back. "I'd just up and go across the sea if I could, head over to Creila or something, but I can't even travel without some kind of restriction. If I'd done something to deserve it, I'd understand, but nope."

"You say that, but looking at you, I'd guess you have a problem. Cutting your hair short so the red won't show up too much? It's not helping. I can see the gleam of magic in your eyes." Cami watched as Dominique drained the second glass. "You going to go for another?"

"Maybe." Dominique considered downing one after the other until she couldn't think straight anymore. Cami was right, after all. Her love for her own power showed in her features, tainting both her hair and eyes. It was the tell-tale sign of any Ilia who had fallen victim to the addictive properties of their own magic.

Though she'd always told herself that magic would never consume her, it had just been a lie. Looking down at the glass, she relented. "Yeah, actually. One more."

Cami gave it to her. Dominique tipped her head back with the glass this time, making the most of the taste, of the burn.

"So," Cami said. "What brings you here, anyway? Apart from the rumour that you might be able to burn matchsticks in peace, of course."

Dominique gave an exaggerated shrug. There were too many ways of answering that question, but all of them felt like she was baring too much of her soul. "Suppose you could say that it's the six-month anniversary of something big."

"Ah, so you're celebrating?"

"Hard to say." She thought of Caspian, of how she'd left him sat on the windowsill, staring through the glass like he might find a purpose in the burnt evening sky. He certainly hadn't been celebrating. "Maybe it'd be easier if I was. Hey, bartenders are supposed to be wise, right?"

"So I've heard. Never met one that seemed that smart though."

Dominique smiled, a grim thing that didn't quite meet her eyes. "So, let's talk relationships. What's your opinion? On friendships, romances, that kind of thing?"

Cami brought a finger to her lips as she pondered the question. The bar continued to shift around them, people coming and going.

Burn it down, whispered Dominique's magic once more, a mosquito of a sound.

"I'd say it's all fun and games, but you're looking for a more interesting answer, aren't you?" Cami said, looking thoughtful. "I think in any kind of relationship, you need to be a pillar of stability for each other, or it can all end up a mess. It's all about finding the right guy, I reckon. What about you?"

"I think a relationship is like a fire," Dominique said, and in her memory, she saw a blaze tear apart the house she'd once called her home. "No single one is equal to another. Some burn bright, some barely get off the ground, but they all burn out eventually. Doesn't matter, though. At some point, they were all the same. Beautiful. Alive. Warm."

"Been burnt before? Is this a happy anniversary, or not?"

"It's an anniversary I'd give anything to forget."

Dominique pushed the empty glass away. Her fingers were too hot; she'd melt it if she wasn't careful. Six months ago today, she and Caspian had been running through the streets as if their lives depended on it.

Standing up, she turned her back on Cami, preparing to leave. "I've had enough. I came looking for a distraction, but maybe it was just a mistake. All I can hear in my head is this…this buzzing. Ilia problem. You wouldn't understand."

Whatever Cami might have said in response was drowned out by the sound of The Otherground's doors slamming open. A young man still in his work uniform came running in, his face was bright red. Everyone went quiet at his presence, startled by the sudden noise.

"Something's happening in Ardr-end!" he shouted, half out of breath. "There's smoke comin' up from everywhere, you can see it from here. Looks like it's been going on for a while!"

That got people moving. With the quiet moment shattered, everyone started clamouring, rushing out or asking questions. Dominique followed the flow of the crowd, her curiosity sparked in a morbid fashion. She knew better than most what smoke meant.

Cami came too as Dominique made her way out onto the sordid

streets of Caul-end. Despite the heavy wall of heat, the air felt charged, like electricity surged through it. The night sky was awash with smoke, more orange than it had been when she walked into the bar. Even though the light from the streetlamps was sub-par as best, she could still see the plume coming up from the other district, huge and magnificent.

"Sweet splits above," Cami breathed beside her. "That looks bad."

Dominique stared, her heartbeat picking up in her chest. The smoke called out to her, beckoning her to come closer. Her nails dug into her palms as she clenched her fists.

"Looking at that smoke, looks like it's near Mellingdale," someone said from behind her. "Maybe it even *is* Mellingdale."

"Mellingdale?" a woman said. "That's some bad luck. Weren't it only recently it had that bad fire?"

"Yeah, most people managed to get out of that one, but I think some guy died. Same one who set it."

Dizziness struck Dominique like a punch to the gut. For a moment, she wasn't outside The Otherground, but instead, in Ardr-end, in Mellingdale, in the house where they had all lived together. Caspian was sat on the sofa, hugging his knees, but she was in another man's lap, his hands ghosting over her shoulders, her arms.

The promise of fire glinted in his gaze even back then. He'd always been dangerous. She'd known it, but she'd ignored the signs.

"I love you," he whispered into her ear. Even his breath was hot. "Say it back. I want to hear it."

"I love you," she replied, because she'd been young and stupid, because she'd meant it.

Someone bashed into her side, jolting her back into the present, the seconds stretching into infinity as she watched more smoke spill into the air. Magic screeched in her ears. *Burn it down.*

A single name fell from her lips, lost to the noise around her. "Ezra?"

But it was impossible, because Ezra was dead.

"Sweetheart?" Cami said. "You still there?"

It had been six months since Mellingdale had burned, and she'd not been back since. It was the place where Ezra had wound her and Caspian around himself like string to a spool before tearing them apart. It had been where they'd lived together, loved together, broke together, right up until Ezra had started a fire that even he couldn't control.

They'd run from him that night, and as far as they knew, he'd died in his own flames.

"Hey, Dominique?" Cami tried again. "Firecracker?"

Dominique's hands shook. Six months to the day and Mellingdale was on fire again. It wasn't a coincidence. There was no possible way that it could be a coincidence.

"I have to go," she said, and then she was running, past the crowds, through the streets. The smoke was her beacon, and she had no choice but to follow it.

She had to know.

CHAPTER 3

By the time Caspian noticed the smoke rising in the distance, it had already begun to engulf the red-hued sky.

His anxiety escaped him in cold bursts as he sat in the corner of the windowsill, his power beyond his own control. The little place that he and Dominique called home was had dropped well below average room temperature, especially for this time of year, but it hardly made a difference to him. He didn't feel the effects of the cold anymore, much less his own magic.

From what he could see, the smoke in the city was far enough away to be of no threat, and yet he couldn't help but consider the possibility that Dominique was the source. Elementras with an affinity for fire were so easily engulfed by their own power. He'd seen it first hand, and he'd noticed the way she'd been looking at her own flames lately. It reminded him of Ezra in the worst possible way.

He knew he couldn't just sit there and wait for it all to blow over, but he found it difficult to make himself move. His mind ran riot, his breath coming rapidly, his heart a fraction too fast. Lifting his hands, Caspian channelled his magic through them, drawing water from his fingertips to manipulate it into a perfect globe.

He peered into the reflective surface. It was a bad habit, but years of terrible influences meant that it was a difficult one to break. Using his power had ruined his appearance, leaving his brown hair streaked through with pale, blue-white strands, while his eyes were icier than ever. When he saw himself in the water's reflection, he couldn't help but realise that he looked more like his late mother than ever.

Ezra had taught him this coping method. "Put it in the water," he'd laugh, taking Caspian by the wrist, his fingers leaving burning impressions. "You act fragile, but I bet that weak spine of yours can take so much more. Here, let me show you."

The memory made Caspian sick, but it still had power over him. Looking into the globe, it felt like he was filtering his fear for Dominique through a lens, the emotion not quite belonging to him, but the water instead. This power would kill him eventually, as it did all Ilia, but, for him, it was impossible to stop.

Looking back to Aquiline, he found it worse than before. The city looked as if it was suffocating beneath the smog, drowning under its weight. With a wave of his hands, the sphere dissipated, and finally, he found it in him to stand up. If something was happening, then maybe he could prove himself for once. He'd already failed them both by not going out with Dominique tonight, but if she was at the site of the fire, then maybe he could still help.

Grabbing his keys, he left the apartment in a rush. Aquiline felt off-kilter as he pushed through it, like the entire world had slanted sideways to accommodate for the fire. He passed by beggars, drunkards, people just trying to get home or away from the chaos. Everyone seemed fearful, unsure, uncertain, and it affected him in turn. Though it was horribly humid, the air around him grew cooler.

As he searched for the source of the smoke, he realised it had to be coming from Ardr-end. Aquiline's eastern-most district wasn't far by train, but he didn't have the cash to take it. Instead, he picked up the pace, hoping he'd be able to get there in time to make any kind of difference. If Dominique wasn't involved, then she would be coming home to an empty house, but he couldn't just stand by and let things run their course.

It was just how he was. Caspian never had been able to ignore a threat. It was what had so often gotten him into trouble when Ezra went rampaging around their house.

Minutes ticked by. The air was so thick with smoke that, by the time he reached Ardr-end's outskirts, he nearly choked on it. Out of breath, he had to stop, doubling over as he tried to force more air into his lungs. The entire district felt electric, like an Elementra with an affinity for lightning was throwing their magic around. Maybe they were.

Looking up, he searched for the smoke's source, only to freeze when he found it. It wasn't far from where he was now, visible even as it grew darker, and as the pieces clicked together, dread gripped hard at his insides.

Mellingdale.

Unable to wait any longer, Caspian set off again, desperate now more than ever to get to the fire's location. He *had* to do something, because no-one would forgive the Ilia if civilians died in the blaze. Once again, their reputation was on the line, every new incident making the public's opinion of them sour further. There had to be a way to salvage the situation, a way to help.

The crowds were huge when he arrived in the neighbourhood, but the fire itself was bigger. It had engulfed more than just their old street, so much ablaze that it was difficult to tell if anything would even be left when it was over. Countless water-based Elementras were already at the scene, tossing what they could at the fire, but their power was nothing in the face of something this wild. Aquiline's sub-par firefighters had arrived too, but their awkward, horse-drawn pumps hardly made a dent.

He tugged up his sleeve, making sure that everyone would be able to see his bracelet. "I can help! Let me through!"

"Caspian?" Dominique's voice surprised him. He looked, and found her amongst the crowd of other Elementras, her eyes wide. Relief flooded him, replacing the dread. Both of them shoved their way through the crowd, grabbing each other by the arms as they made contact.

"What are you doing here?" he asked, needing to shout to be heard over the roar of colliding magic. "This wasn't you, right?"

She shook her head. "No! I saw it from Caul-end and came to see if I could help. You too?"

"Yeah. Can you calm the flames?"

"They're not natural, it's no normal fire. I can't control them, look!"

As she raised her hands, Caspian saw flames spark at her fingertips. Usually, she had full control over any kind of fire, able to snuff them out or make them grow with a simple, silent command. Not here. This fire ignored her as if it had a will of its own.

Dropping her hands back to her sides, she gave him a desperate look. "There's nothing I can do, Caspy. I don't know how to stop it."

Looking between the raging fire and the line of water Elementras who were trying their best to fight it, Caspian made his decision. They were giving it their all, he could see that much in their faces, but it wasn't enough. Most Ilia weren't like him or Dominique; the amount of power one could control varied, but the two of them were more powerful than average. It came at a cost; though most Ilia would live long lives alongside their magic, Caspian wasn't sure if he'd even see his twentieth birthday in a couple of months.

"We need to suffocate the fire," Caspian said. The heat was beginning to get to him, his natural power unable to counteract it, sapping the strength he needed to draw on. He dashed his arm across his forehead, wiping at the sweat. "I know you can't control the flames, but do you think you can do something about the heat?"

Dominique nodded, offering a small smile. "Who do you think I am, Caspy? Of course I can."

They parted, him going to join the line of water Elementras while she approached the fire. Taking a steadying breath, he began to focus his power, searching for the threads of it that he knew thrived within him.

It began in his chest, like a tidal wave in his ribcage. It flowed outwards, surfacing at his fingertips. There was so little moisture in the air that it was more difficult than usual, so he took what he could and then turned to the Elementras around him. He could use them to bolster his own magic, so he did. Dragging their power from them, he made it his own.

Water gathered above them in response, a whirlpool made from near nothing. The other Elementras noticed his efforts and began to further their own, joining their magic with his willingly, his power growing. Silently, he thanked them, knowing now more than ever that he had to give it his all. With precision only the most skilled of his kind would be capable of, he directed the whirlpool towards the blaze, and when it was in place, he let it free.

It erupted, coating the flames in its downpour. Once wouldn't be enough, so he drew on his magic again, revelling in the feeling, everyone around him doing their best to help him kill the fire. He doubted any of them had the permission to be doing this—he certainly didn't have a license—but there was no time to think about it. He could only hope an exception would be made at the end of it all. Aquiline always tried to regulate its magic to the strictest degree, but surely this was different.

As they worked, more Elementras joined their efforts. Those with an affinity for wind came to stop the fire from spreading. Other water Elementras leant their power to Caspian. Dominique contained the heat, so he could only hope that it would all come together. He just had to keep the downpour up.

Slowly, it began to lessen. With each area they cleared, they moved on, every drop of water bringing them closer to the end. Caspian didn't think about it, he simply was. That was how it was with magic. It embodied him as he embodied it.

It wasn't kind, though. As more of the fire died down to flickering embers, he nearly fell to his knees. Magic gave, but it also took, and the aftershocks of his power would be hitting any moment now. He looked for Dominique, but she didn't seem to be nearby. Trusting that she would have left the area, Caspian decided not to stick around either, to let the others deal with the little that remained. He didn't want to be there when the Ilpolitia started grabbing every Ilia for questioning. He had no energy to give them answers.

Around him, the other Ilia were still coming down from using their power, some still throwing their water around to try and keep the fire from reigniting. It made for good cover. He used the disorder to escape, but though he wanted to be out of Mellingdale entirely, his body wasn't going to let him get that far. He made it a little way from the scene before losing his balance, going down hard on his knees.

Pain built up in his blood, ice cold, the only kind he ever really felt anymore. He bit back the scream in his throat and tried to breathe as his magic rebelled against him. The pressure made it feel like his chest would explode. Nothing worked against it, and all he wished was that Dominique was with him.

This was the consequence of using his power. A strangled gasp escaped his throat as another wave of pain struck him. It felt like decay inside, like his own body was rotting. He grasped at the concrete, at the ferns that had sprung up through the sidewalk, and shut his eyes.

"You're not okay, are you?"

Someone else was with him, but Caspian didn't have it in him to look up. Masculine voice, upper-class accent, just like a Nadre-ender. Caspian couldn't focus. He could only continue to grip the ferns.

Footsteps, slow, considered. The other person stood over him, and when Caspian finally made himself look, he saw a young man illuminated by the shoddy light of the streetlamp. A youthful lad, maybe only Caspian's age or slightly younger, with light brown hair cropped close to his head. His boyish features made it difficult to tell his exact age. Maybe he simply hadn't grown out of them yet.

"I saw you," he said. "You were out there, fighting the fire, but you were more powerful than the others. How did you do that?"

Caspian couldn't reply. He could barely think.

"Hey," the other man said. Caspian hoped that, if he didn't reply, he'd go away. No such luck. "Those other Ilia, they weren't nearly as impressive. Me and my friend couldn't take our eyes off you."

Finding his voice, Caspian asked, "Who are you?"

"The people around here call me Kinglet," the young man replied. It wasn't his real name, Caspian could glean that much, but he didn't have it in him to question it. "I was passing through when the fire broke out, but I'm not anyone special."

"You just stopped and watched?"

"What else could I do? If I'd have left, that'd just make me some callous bastard, right?" Kinglet knelt down beside him. "You're from around here, right? I saw how you charged in, looking so desperate. You knew someone in those houses?"

Caspian shook his head. The pain felt a little further away now, like it was beginning to subside. He knew better than to believe that it was the end of it. "I used to live here. Not anymore. Why did you follow me?"

"No real reason." Kinglet waited a second before standing up again, hands in his pockets. He wore a heavy looking messenger bag over his white, button up shirt. "You should get up."

Caspian couldn't, not just yet, not with his legs feeling so weak. "Why?"

"Because I say so," Kinglet said. "Look, you seem in way worse a state than those other Ilia, and Rian told me to…" he trailed off, shaking his head. "Never mind. You know what? This is stupid. I shouldn't have bothered. I'm leaving."

"No, wait." Caspian didn't know why he said it. He hadn't even wanted to speak to this guy in the first place, but now he was curious as to the real reason why Kinglet had gone out of his way to follow him. "I'm coming, just give me a moment."

He got to his feet slowly, feeling Kinglet's gaze on him the entire time. After a moment, he spoke. "Listen, I don't want to give off the wrong impression. What I'm doing here, this is a one-time deal, alright? Where do you live?"

Telling a stranger the exact location didn't seem like the best of plans, especially when Caspian had gone through enough trouble with people he *had* trusted in the past. "Just Caul-end. Why do you care?"

"I don't. How are you getting back?"

Caspian hadn't thought about it. Now he did, he realised it was going to have to be on foot, a prospect that wasn't entirely inviting given his current state. "I'm walking it."

Kinglet raised his eyebrows. "Oh, sure you are, because you're going to get *so* far when you look half dead. Are you going to let me help you to the station, or not?"

"What? I can't afford the train."

"One good deed deserves another, or so the saying goes. I don't put much stock in it, nor do I actually care either way, but my best friend keeps going on at me to be a better person. So here it is; I'm being a better person, and that's no word of a lie either. I'll pay for your train if you want me to help, so will you follow me or not?"

Caspian hesitated, the other man's disposition difficult to understand. It was like he ran hot and then cold, as if even Kinglet *himself* wasn't sure of how he was supposed to be coming across. After a half second of debate, Caspian's desire to get back home won out over any perceived threat. "Alright, I'm coming."

He had ways of protecting himself if anything was to go wrong. Kinglet was in more danger than Caspian was, he just had to remember that.

One of Kinglet's hands rested in his pocket as they made their way through the streets, the other toying with the strap of his bag. In the better light, Caspian was able to make out more of his face, his eyes bright green, his eyebrows drawn together in a frown. He didn't look happy, but then again, it seemed like he was intentionally making his feelings difficult to discern. Though they'd been in each other's company for several minutes now, Caspian still had no idea what he was thinking.

"I don't understand," he said, because the night was in shambles and he'd lost track of it somewhere between leaving his home and arriving at the site of the fire. Kinglet offered up no kind of explanation, so Caspian was left alone with his thoughts.

He hoped Dominique was okay, wherever she'd gone.

Kinglet led him to the nearest station. It was dead outside, and he could only assume that everyone who would have normally had been there had scattered in the wake of the fire. There was *one* young man waiting out front, though, a short lad with blond hair and rougher clothing than Kinglet. Everything he wore frayed at the edges, short sleeves losing threads, hems coming undone.

When he spotted them, he gave a cheery wave. "Well, look at this! Our Wren, actually going out and extending a helping hand for once!"

Kinglet narrowed his eyes. "*Rian.*"

Rian grinned, giving Caspian a once-over. "Glad to see he helped you out. I thought he weren't gonna, that he'd just up and ignore what I said, but look at him now! It was me who put him up to it, you know? Whatever he told you about this shtick, it was probably bull-shit, he does that a lot."

"Uh," Caspian said, searching for something, anything, to respond with. "Wren? I knew you were lying about that weird name."

"It's not weird," Wren said.

"It's a nickname," Rian said directly over him. When Wren shot him a sharp look, he laughed. "Call him whatever you feel better with, he don't mind much."

Wren's expression suggested that he very much minded, but Caspian wasn't one for false monikers. Not that it mattered, when there were more pressing questions to be asked. "Rian, was it? Have you seen a woman come through here? Her name is Dominique, she's an Elementra like me, and she was helping with the fire."

Rian looked at Wren in question, only to receive a shrug in response. "Apparently not, mate. Just you. We thought you looked pretty damn determined to stop that fire, so I told Wren to help you out. Well, dared him, more like. I thought it'd be a nice thing to do, right? Not like I have the cash to help."

"You just wanted an excuse to spend my money," Wren muttered, but he was smiling too now.

Rian slapped him on the back, gesturing to the station's doors with his other hand. "Well, whatever, let's see this unlikely hero off home. He really gave it his all, huh? Why not give him a little extra to get his girl home when she comes by?"

It felt a little bit like charity. Caspian wasn't sure if he deserved it. "You don't have to do that."

But Rian was already ushering him into the station, and Wren had already dug into his bag, grumbling beneath his breath about how Rian was taking the piss now. Wincing, Caspian shook his head, pushing back. "Please, don't worry, really, I can get home."

"No, no, it's fine." Wren freed his wallet from his bag and began flipping through it. "Rian won't ever let me hear the end of it if I just let you go, so take it. Something, something, good person, right?"

"Right," Rian agreed, looking delighted. "Now we've got a train to catch too, so you have a nice night now, yeah?"

Wren shoved the money into Caspian's grip, and then the two of them were gone before he could even utter a thank you. He stood there, the cash in hand, utterly dumbfounded. It didn't feel real. The notes felt like they might disintegrate at any moment.

But it *was* real. The entire night had been real. He looked down at the money and tried to wrap his head around it all. The fire, the anniversary, Wren and Rian and their whirlwind appearances. Maybe it meant nothing at all, but it didn't feel insignificant.

Was there a meaning to it all? Why had Mellingdale burned again? He wouldn't find the answers in a dingy Ardr-end train station. Dominique had to be around somewhere, so he pocketed the cash and headed back out to find her. They had a way home now, and he couldn't wait to tell her.

CHAPTER 4

DOMINIQUE TURNED THE THICK, HEAVY TOME IN HER HANDS, EXAMINING the cover that barely clung onto the book after so many years of life. Cracked and imperfect, it was hardly the most beautiful of books, but that was why she'd taken an interest in it to begin with.

She'd checked it out of Ardr-end's most prestigious library about a week ago after having dipped her head in out of interest. The old, cumbersome book had been hidden behind many more modern books, the title long since faded away, but a quick flip through had revealed it to be full of ancient Ilia tales. Because Dominique had always liked ugly books, she'd decided to take it home, though only one of the stories had ended up being of any interest to her. Her bookmark still sat inside, marking it out for her to reread before she took it back.

Beside her, on the other bed, Caspian still slept. They'd arrived home the night before utterly exhausted, the only blessing having been the money that Caspian's mystery helpers had gifted him. She hadn't quite believed the story when he told her. Too much alcohol on her part, she thought, but no. He insisted it to be true.

"Caspy," she said quietly. "Want to hear about the story I'm reading?"

He stirred, muttering something beneath his breath. The early morning light spilled in through the window, making the brown that was still left in his hair look golden. Sitting on the side of his bed, she nudged him gently. "Come on, I know you worked hard last night, but you must have had enough sleep by now."

Blearily, he opened his eyes. "Never enough. Felt like a dream, all of last night…did it really happen?"

"Unfortunately." Dominique dropped the book on his bedside table when he didn't show any interest. She'd been trying to distract herself from the memory of the fire, but it kept repeating on her like some putrid aftertaste. How beautiful that blaze had looked as it tore Mellingdale apart. How sick it was that she thought that.

"I was hoping it had been just a nightmare," Caspian said as he sat up. "Maybe it doesn't mean anything. Fires happen all the time, right?"

"Yeah," Dominique went to her drawers, hunting through for her clothes. "We both know it's more than that, though. Someone started that fire, someone who had a reason to burn it all down. We'd be stupid to brush it aside."

Caspian quietened at that. He looked away as she got dressed, even though they'd been living together for years and she was certain he'd seen her in less than just her underwear. When she pulled her trousers on, they felt a little loose around her waist, something she didn't want to linger on.

Finally, Caspian said, "It's not possible. He's dead."

He sounded far away as he said that, and she felt guilty for even planting the idea in his mind. She couldn't help but voice it, though, because she'd been considering that explanation ever since she'd seen smoke rising from outside The Otherground.

"Is he, Caspian? Or is that just what we wanted to believe?" Her tone sounded almost hopeful, and she hated herself for it. Caspian didn't meet her eyes when she looked at him, but at his fingertips, she saw the glimmer of magic.

Her feelings were difficult to put into words, but there was a part of her that missed Ezra Purnell. Before he'd become the obsessive, controlling man they'd run from, there had been inside jokes, passionate nights, games, dinners, more. She knew Caspian felt the same. That was why he was staring down at his hands like he was about to pull a sphere of water from them.

"There's no way he escaped that fire," he said.

"Then let's make sure," Dominique said, grabbing her bag. "You get dressed, I'll make breakfast. We'll eat, and then we'll go have a look. I don't think this fire was an accident, but if it wasn't him, then why would someone else burn Mellingdale? There has to be a reason for it, and I want to know."

He didn't look convinced. No, instead, Caspian looked very much like he wanted to turn her down. But he didn't, because that wasn't in his nature and they both knew it. Instead, he looked at her, nodding imperceptibly.

"Alright," he said. "We'll go."

Mellingdale was crammed full of Ilpolitia when they arrived, swarming the streets like city pigeons as they poked their noses into everything, taking people aside for questioning as Dominique and Caspian both did their best to dodge their paths. Their presence instantly confirmed what she'd theorised earlier; the fire hadn't been natural. The Ilpol only showed up for one of two reasons; either an Ilia had been involved in a crime, or a *split*—a gateway to another world—had opened in the vicinity.

She'd heard no news of any otherworldly realms showing up in Ardr-end, so that only meant that an Ilia had committed the crime, exactly as she'd expected.

Caspian didn't look well in the early morning light, the previous evening having taken its toll on him. He was getting worse, just as she was, though neither of them said anything about it. There was nothing *to* say.

"Bloody Ilpol," she said, watching one corner a young woman wearing a yellow bracelet. "What, is every Elementra in Mellingdale a suspect now? Whatever happened to 'innocent 'til proven guilty'?"

"It's just easier for them to assume everyone's got ill intentions," Caspian said.

"Easier, and wrong."

"We all know that, but try telling *them.*"

Parts of the street were cordoned off, but the scorched remains were still obviously visible. According to a paper she'd picked up before they'd left Caul-end, the fire had started at many different points, several people had lost their lives, and the melted badge of an Ilpol officer had been recovered from the debris. Nothing was confirmed yet, the fire had left little in the way of actual human remains, but if an officer *had* died, then things were looking grim for the Ilia.

The Ilpol would never forgive and forget, not when it came back to one of their own.

Though most people around the blockade were shouting at the Ilpol, asking for answers, there were two young men who instead stood back from the crowd and chatted animatedly to each other. She approached and listened in long enough to gather that they were discussing their theories on what the Ilpolitia would do next, which meant they probably knew more than she did.

"Uh, Domi," Caspian whispered urgently. "Those two, they're—!"

Dominique tapped the shorter man of the two on the shoulder, ignoring Caspian's startled yelp. "Excuse me, do you know what happened here?"

The taller man shut up immediately, green eyes narrowing as they focused on her. The shorter one, however, gave her a friendly wave. "Oh, you interested lass? Well, given that pretty red bracelet of yours, I'd say you know exactly what went down here, but hey. I'll tell you anyway. Whole neighbourhood burned down, caused a right big old ruckus it did."

"That's obvious. I actually mean, did you know what *caused* it."

"Of course we do," said the taller man, a smug looking grin on his face. "Why, we were out here last night, just passing by like ordinary men do, when we saw this young woman with a bracelet—"

"Yeah, yeah, no need to be an asshole, Wren," the shorter one butted in. "He gets a kick out of making shit up, so don't mind him. Ilpol are saying it's an Elementra, but let's be real, that's just fancy talk for 'arsonist'. Truth is, nobody knows for sure, and they're gonna blame an Ilia no matter what."

The taller of the two looked past her then, raising his eyebrows. "Look, Rian, what a coincidence. It's the Elementra from last night. Found your girlfriend then?"

Dominique looked behind her to where Caspian was stood. He'd tried and failed to make it look like he wasn't paying attention, staring solidly off to the side.

"She's not my girlfriend," he said.

"You know these clowns?" Dominique asked.

He shrugged. "Kind of. Wren was the one who paid for us to get the train home last night."

"Yeah, after I basically held him at gunpoint," the shorter one—Rian—said cheerfully. "He's stingy as anything, he is, but I can always get through to him."

Wren rolled his eyes. "Remind me why we're friends again?"

"Because you'd be right lonely without me chattering your ear off. Anyway—" Rian stepped forward, closing the gap between them and Dominique. "What's wrong, lass? You look a bit pale. Is it the neighbourhood? Looks pretty bad, don't it? Ilpol are saying a little girl died, and some old couple too, and there's also that Ilpol officer who's missing. They found a body, you know, but it's unrecognizable. All that was left was his badge."

Wren let out a low whistle. "The Ilia are screwed."

"Yeah. Anyway, lass, you're the one asking us, but I think it's fair to throw the question back. Do *you* know anything about what happened here?"

"Maybe," she said. It looked too similar to before, the destruction absolute, everything swallowed whole by the fire. "Reminds me of something else."

Caspian looked at the destruction too, his expression unreadable. "We were caught up in a fire half a year ago, just like this. It seemed too close for comfort, so we wanted to check in case there were any clues left behind…in case it was the same person who did it."

Rian hummed. "Well, is it?"

"I don't think so."

"Then why the long faces? Got nothing to do with you, right? Honestly, it ain't got anything to do with us either, we were just passing through when it happened and we wanted to come back and see if anything had changed. That said, I'm definitely interested now. I love a good mystery, I do. Hey, lass, what's your name?"

"Domi," she replied. "And this is Caspian."

"I know that, remember? Anyway, I'm Rian, Rian McCarrick. You might have heard of me?" He paused expectantly, but Dominique and Caspian could only answer him with a shake of their heads. Wren pressed his hand to his face, looking mildly irritated, but it didn't deter Rian at all. "Oh. You don't? Weird. I'm well known 'round Caulend 'cause I'm good at getting information. People like me, see?"

"Can't imagine why," Wren said, lowering his hand with a wry smile.

"It's 'cause I'm more inviting than you, you uptight, dishonest snob," Rian said, punching his arm gently. "Hey, Domi, you know The Otherground?"

Finally, a subject that she was somewhat comfortable with. "Yeah, I was there last night actually."

"Great! Me and Wren love that place. Tell you what, I'll see if I can dig up any extra info for you on what caused this fire, and I'll meet you there to tell you all about it. Will that wipe those sad looks off your faces?"

It would, but the way he was offering wasn't comforting. Nothing in Aquiline ever came for free, especially when it was regular folk bartering with an Ilia. Eyeing him suspiciously, she asked, "Why would you help us?"

"Well, 'cause it's good practice, right? Like I said, I love a good mystery, and this'll be a nice story for my dad. He ain't too well right now and he loves hearing about the shit I get up to, so I don't wanna disappoint him." Rian's smile was all teeth. "Let's say tonight. Meet me at The Otherground and I'll share whatever we've found, that good for you?"

Wren gave him a hideous look. "Are you serious? We're going to waste our day getting information for veritable *strangers*? Please tell me you're pulling my leg. I've done enough for these two already!"

"You don't have to come, though I'd prefer it if you did. C'mon, Wren, it'll be way more fun if you're messing with people!"

The two began bickering amongst themselves. Dominique couldn't believe they had the gall to argue in public like this. Both of them felt larger than life, ridiculous and completely unreal.

Looking at Caspian, she whispered, "Do you really know these idiots?"

"I only met them last night," he replied helplessly.

"*Anyway*," Rian cut Wren off in the middle of an angry tirade. "We've got places to be, people to see, information to figure out, all that. We'll be off!"

"You're really going to stick your head out for us?" Dominique asked.

"It's called spontaneity, lass, or, something like that. Point is, life is meaningless, so we might as well make some fun out of it." Rian stopped short when he realised that Wren had already started walking away. Giving a wave, he made to catch up. "See ya!"

Dominique stared at their retreating backs wordlessly. Caspian tilted his head. "They were...just as weird as they were last night, actually."

"Yeah. They really paid for you to go home?"

"For some reason." He turned and gestured down the street. "It was just past there; I was getting over the aftershocks when that Wren guy crept up on me and asked if I was okay. I don't think he really under-stood, but...yeah, he took me back to the station and shoved the money at me while Rian kept going on about how he'd put him up to it. I don't get them at all."

Neither did she. Eccentricity was one thing, but she wasn't sure if that was quite it. "I doubt they'll find anything on their little hunt, but I guess it can't hurt to meet up with them again, even if they are kind of weird."

"As long as the Ilpol don't grab them for snooping first," Caspian said, tugging her back by the arm when they both clocked a duo of officers walking past. "We should get out of here. They're probably going to be knocking on our door any day now to ask you questions about all this. Let's not give them any more reason to be suspicious."

Dominique scoffed. He was right, but just because it was Caspian saying it, it didn't make it any less irritating. She'd never not wanted to be an Ilia—it was her lot in life and she'd accepted that—but she sometimes wished that she'd been born elsewhere. Other countries treated their Ilia differently. Across the ocean in Seldist, they were revered. In Creila, they were scarce and ignored. Their country of Harriden was not so lax. Its paranoia led to its flawed regulations, laws that had been hastily put in place and never revised.

But the worst kept secret of Harriden was this; the laws didn't work. A ban on magic would be impossible to enforce given the sheer number of Ilia who called the country home, so instead, the law required them to register themselves. Not everyone did. Magic was a difficult secret to keep, but it didn't stop many from trying.

Some succeeded.

"Should we head home, Caspy?" she said as they made their way back through Mellingdale's cool, overcast streets. "You look tired, and I could do with a rest too before we go and meet those guys."

"Sounds like a good idea," Caspian said. He looked back one last time towards the ruined neighbourhood, prompting her to look back too. As she swept her gaze over the burnt shell of the area she'd once called home, one pervasive thought came back to her, one that refused to be shaken.

Ezra Purnell had caused this fire. Somehow, from beyond the grave or through some other means, this was his doing. The only question was, *how?*

CHAPTER 5

For Caspian, going back home to Caul-end was always a reminder of everything they'd lost.

They hadn't been well-off when they'd lived in Mellingdale, but between the three of them, they'd made it work. Pooling their earnings together, they'd had a roof over their heads and food to eat, helping only each other when Aquiline refused to give them the time of day.

Nowadays, it wasn't so simple. Both he and Dominique were wearing out, and work was getting harder and harder to find. The abilities they could offer were unique, but they required a licence to use them, and neither of them would ever qualify for one given the state they were in. All that was left were laborious odd-jobs that required them to often be in the right place at the right time, and even when they did manage to get them, completing them to the satisfaction of their employer was another matter.

Ultimately, after the fire, they'd had no choice but to settle down in the dumping ground of Aquiline; Caul-end. Their two-room home was barely furnished, and most of their money went towards the rent and keeping themselves fed. The little rest they saved in the hope of one day being able to escape, but the jar was half-empty rather than half-full in terms of coins.

In the hours after their meeting with Rian, they killed the time by playing cards in their grungy half-living room, half kitchen. Opening the windows didn't do much to rid the room of its dry, stuffy heat, and so Caspian focused more on exuding cool air than actually trying to win. With every loss, Dominique came up with a new game, but his focus was shot and he could barely keep up with her bizarre rules.

"If I didn't know any better, I'd say you were losing on purpose," she said, scooping up her pile of cards as she won yet another round. "Come on, Caspy, how about you come up with a game?"

"I'm awful at cards," he said, which wasn't a lie. When it became clear that he didn't really have it in him to commit to the games, they both abandoned the cards and fell onto the sofa together. It was an old, worn thing, three cushions wide, with more springs popping out of it than were still contained inside. They took up two spaces by themselves, the third a constant reminder that once, things had been worse.

"You're on edge," Dominique said. "What's wrong, Caspy?"

He closed his eyes. In his ears, his magic whispered, *wash it away.* It nipped at him like an insect, and he knew that, one day, he would drown in that voice. "I'm just tired."

It was hardly the greatest of excuses and they both knew it. He heard Dominique shift. "You're upset about Mellingdale too, right?"

Upset was hardly the right word, not when his insides were so twisted up in hatred and anger. "I just don't like being reminded of the past."

"Ezra, you mean," Dominique said. The magic rose its voice in response to that name, hissing, *wash him away.*

Quiet descended over them both. Eventually, he fell asleep, but he didn't rest well. Caspian's dreams were full of fire, the ghost of a dead man, and uncomfortable, raging heat. When Dominique shook him awake hours later, their meeting with Rian imminent, his focus remained shot. Shaky and irritated, the last thing he wanted to do was go out, but they'd made a deal. He couldn't just not go.

To his relief, The Otherground wasn't far from where they lived. It was a dingy looking tavern on a dingy looking street, the light low and the company skeevy. The presence of other Ilia was of little comfort, even if they were the only sort he ever felt at home with.

Inside, at least, The Otherground was more welcoming, pleasantly warm unlike their home, and the smell of hot food was always inviting. Behind the bar, a handsome, rugged man cleaned glasses, and sat at the counter was Rian himself. He held a mug of something frothy and alcoholic-looking despite the fact that he barely seemed old enough to drink.

He waved at them when he clocked them, looking absolutely delighted. "You made it! Come over, come over, don't be shy, yeah?"

Dominique glanced past him to the man behind the counter. "Hey, is the woman from the other night not here? Cami, I mean."

Caspian wished he'd come by the previous night just to understand who she was talking about. Rian took a swig from his mug and laughed. "Dane ain't good enough for you? Oi, Dane! You hear that? Lass don't like you none."

"That's not it!" Dominique said as Dane raised his eyebrows. "It's just that she was alright, and I wanted my friend to say hi to her."

Dane put down the glass he'd been cleaning and gestured for her to sit. "Yeah, well, you won't have to wait long. She's out the back dealing with a scuffle 'cause some Ilia picked a fight with Kinglet."

"Hah! Don't give Wren that much credit." Rian's grin betrayed his amusement. Turning back to Dominique, he said, "Our Wren tried swindling the wrong guy and got into an argument. Didn't see much of what happened before Cami hauled them out of here, but it was definitely his fault."

"He's not doing his reputation any favours, that's for sure," Dane said. "So, anyway, you're the firecracker that Cami mentioned. She said you were Domi, and that makes your friend…?"

Dominique nudged him when Caspian failed to respond. "Introduce yourself."

"Oh, uh, yeah. I'm Caspian." He sat down on a nearby stall, only to jump when Rian waved his hand in front of his face. "What?"

"Can't have that one, that seat's spoken for, mate," he said, only to shake his head when Caspian went to stand again. "Nah, it's okay, actually. Suppose you can keep it 'til Wren comes back, seeing as you seem to want it so bad."

Caspian didn't really want the seat at all, but now he felt trapped on it. Dominique took the stall next to him, and Rian downed the rest of his drink. An uncomfortable silence settled over the three of them, none of them offering anything up first. The awkwardness was stifling.

"So!" Rian slammed his mug down onto the counter just as it reached breaking point. "You two get up to anything fun while we were off running about?"

"We played cards," Dominique replied.

"Oh, I like cards, I do. Wren's real great at 'em, got the best poker face and can bluff into infinity. But that's beside the point, ain't it?" Rian smiled. He always seemed to be armed with one. Caspian wondered what lay behind it.

"What *is* your point then?" Caspian asked.

Rian's grin only grew wider. "Well, I got some info, of course! About you guys for starts. Now, Dominique Delacroix, that's a name you don't easily forget, huh?"

Caspian noticed that she was bouncing her leg, drumming her fingertips against the counter. "Okay, you got my last name from someone. So?"

"So nothing. I just thought it was interesting. That's a Creilish surname, but I don't hear no accent on you. You from there, then? If so, why come to Harriden? You heard about how grand we treat our Ilia and decided you'd be better off here?"

She gave him a withering glare. "My great-grandparents moved here or something. It was before Ilia magic showed up in our blood-line. I don't know, does it matter?"

Rian laughed, gesturing at Dane for a refill. "Nah, why would it? I just like getting the scope of things, is all. Anyway, the people 'round Ardr-end really seemed to know about you, and Caspian here too. Heard all about the ways you guys got into trouble." He paused while Dane filled his mug to the brim. "Had some issues with a past boyfriend, Domi?"

She looked away from him. "That's none of your business."

Caspian started to regret ever accepting Rian's help. The last thing they needed was some stranger poking around in their history. "Can we just stick to the fire? Our past is in the past for a reason. We're not here to revisit it like that."

"Right, right! Sorry, I just like picking apart the details." Rian picked up his newly filled mug, but didn't drink from it. Instead, he sloshed the liquid from side to side with his animated gestures. "It's kind of my thing, you know? I love figuring out why people do what they do, motive, all that crap. Don't you think it's fun?"

Caspian hardly cared either way. He was starting to get the feeling that Rian could talk for the entirety of Aquiline if they let him. Though he had a magnetic quality about him that made him seem approachable, all it did was set Caspian further on edge. Ezra had been the same, charismatic, fun, and charming. It was why they'd stayed with him for so long, why they'd let so many things go without complaint.

People with that kind of influence were dangerous, and Caspian didn't know how aware of his power Rian was.

Before either he or Dominique could offer up a reply, a woman entered from a door behind the counter. Wren was with her, arms crossed, a black-and-blue bruise forming on his cheek. The entire right side of his face looked decidedly awful, and his fury-ridden expression didn't help him much either.

Rian gawked at him. "Shit, Kinglet, that Empathra *punched* you? Your parents are gonna have a fit, weren't you meant to be going down to the Juebury theatre tonight?"

The look Wren shot him was utterly poisonous.

"Are you badgering my customers, McCarrick?" the woman asked as Wren hopped over the counter. "Oh, Dominique! You look better tonight. Who's your friend?"

"His name's Caspian, Cami," Rian said over the top of them. "And he's just moving, ain't he?"

Caspian hurriedly began to get up, but Wren said, "No, it's fine. I'll sit somewhere else."

He didn't sit in the end, instead perching on the edge of the counter. Caspian would have rather given up the seat and taken that spot, but the look Dane and Cami gave each other suggested that it was something that only Wren would get away with. As the two of them left to attend to their other customers, Dominique leant forward, her expression carefully blank.

"So," she said. "Fire. Mellingdale. What did you find out?"

"A lot of poppycock, and absolutely nothing interesting," Wren said, inspecting his own hand. Rian watched him intently, like Wren was the only other person in the bar, like he was all that mattered. Caspian recognized that expression on his face; it was one that Dominique had so often directed at Ezra. It was one that Caspian often directed at *Dominique.*

But what did it mean in their context? They weren't them. The same rules didn't apply. It seemed that Wren didn't understand it either. He noticed Rian staring and glanced over. "What?"

"Liar," Rian said.

"Well, it wasn't interesting to *me.*"

Rian sighed, finally looking back to Caspian and Dominique. "Don't listen to Kinglet, he loves twisting the truth to get a rise out of people. We *did* get something. As it turns out, someone seems to be looking for you two down in Ardr-end. When I mentioned your names, people got right shifty, they did."

Caspian's stomach turned. His magic whispered, *wash it away.* Drawing on it in public was inexcusable, he knew, but oh, how he wanted to. What Rian said didn't bode well; he and Dominique kept to themselves, and there was nobody else they knew well in Aquiline. There was only one person he could think of who might be looking for them, but it couldn't be true.

"Anyway, that's not the main deal," Rian continued, the warm light of The Otherground making him look softer than he truly was. "I did some more digging after that, and we found out that these chaps *did* see someone suspicious last night; a registered fire Elementra that looked like death. And get this! He's the one who's been mooching about looking for you guys. The man I spoke to said to me that they've been trying to get the Ilpol to look into him for ages, but they wouldn't listen 'cause the Elementra was meant to be dead."

Dominique didn't react, her expression unreadable.

"You didn't say where we were, right?" Caspian said quickly. Panic twisted his voice into a pathetic thing. "You didn't mention us at all, right? Right?"

"Of course we told them. How else would we get the information?" Wren said.

Caspian's throat went dry. Dominique started to get up.

"Woah, woah, calm down," Rian said, giving Wren a tight look. Wren ignored it entirely. "Tch, asshole...look, you two, I'm gonna tell you one thing about Kinglet; don't believe a word out of his mouth. We didn't say nothing, trust me, he's just trying to mess with you 'cause he's pissed about getting punched."

"Now I know why Dane said you have a bad reputation," Dominique said to Wren, keeping her voice admirably even. Wren gave a haughty laugh, but said nothing in return. "I don't care what you did or didn't say, but I want to know, did you find out who was asking after us? A name? A face?"

"They wouldn't tell me. Said they were scared he'd hear they'd been saying his name and that he'd come after their places next. All they said was he was some fire-starter Elementra." Rian finished up his drink for the second time, planting the mug back on the counter. "You know who it is, don't you? I can see it on your faces. You both look bloody terrified."

It wasn't true. They'd spent the last six months hiding from Ezra's memory, trying to heal, trying to forget. Caspian's hand ghosted across his side, where, beneath the thin fabric of his shirt, scarring remained. Ezra was dead, he tried to tell himself. He'd died in the fire.

But the Ilpolitia had never recovered a body, had they?

"There's something else, isn't there?" he said. "Tell me you have something else. Anything."

"Maybe just one more thing," Rian said. "I went a little further for you, just 'cause I'm a nice guy and all."

Wren cringed. "People who say they're 'nice guys' are usually anything but."

"Yeah, you'd know, wouldn't you?" Rian snickered. "Anyway, *as I was saying*, I asked around. Other people have seen this Elementra, and apparently he's somehow cobbling it together and staying in

Ardr-end. See? The good ol' Ilpol should just hire me. I've gotten more info in a day then they could probably gather in a week."

Caspian stopped listening. The Otherground felt far away, like a sheet of water separated him and it, like he was looking through its glimmering surface. Wren and Rian looked like the strangers they were, unfamiliar and unknown, and all he could hear was his magic once more, rising, rising.

Wash it all away.

~

"So," Rian said, stretching his arms out in front of him. "Can I ask something insensitive?"

It had been minutes, or hours. Caspian had been staring off into the distance for some time now while Rian and Wren had chattered amongst themselves and Dominique drew invisible shapes into the countertop with her finger. For Caspian, his thoughts had been lost, filled with images of the bar drenched in water and it took all of him to not give in to the need.

Ilia magic begged to be used. That was its nature.

At Rian's unexpected question, Dominique finally looked up, narrowing her eyes. "Do you interrogate everyone you meet?"

"Only the ones that pique my interest," Rian said, looking as cheery as ever. "Kinglet says it's 'intrusive' and 'rude', but I don't care none. Ain't like he can talk when he's worse than me, but hey. I'm curious, and I like a good chatter, so, can I ask?"

"Wren's actually right on that one." She paused, as if she was considering her answer. Caspian had nothing to say even when she looked to him for permission, so, resting her head on her hand, she said, "Okay, shoot."

Rian finally dropped his smile, his gaze turning sombre. Completely straight-faced, he said, "How long do you two have left, anyway?"

"*Rian!*" Wren stood up, looking appalled. "You can't just ask that!"

Caspian felt cold at the question, shivers rattling his spine. The

41

temperature dropped around them, and in a way, it was the silent answer to Rian's question.

Dominique spoke for them both. "You're a funny one, Wren. Do you care or not? Ten minutes ago you were preying on our fears, now you're pretending that Rian's in the wrong for asking something like that?"

Wren scowled. "Don't get me wrong, I couldn't care less."

"Sure." Dominique sighed, turning her attention back to Rian. "To answer your question, not as long as everyone thinks."

"Well, you look good for it then." Rian grinned at them again. How many other people had he gotten to know intimately just by being brave enough to ask taboo questions? How many secrets did that unguarded smile take? "Tell you what, I'll buy you both drinks. Well, Wren will, 'cause I can't really afford it. Caul-ender, y'know? Comes with my territory."

With a groan, Wren reached into his bag and dragged a handful of coins from it. "I can't believe this," he muttered. "I'm only doing this because you were rude. The bank of Wren Sharp, ever at your service, freeloader. Cami! While I'm being robbed, at least get them drunk in my stead. My parents really will kill me if I go home wasted."

Because Wren was buying, and because Wren seemed entirely self-centred, he chose their drinks without giving them a say. Caspian stared at the glass of wine that was put in front of him, something so ludicrously expensive that he and Dominique would never have been able to afford it on a normal night out.

Not that it mattered. Dominique took a sip and grimaced.

"Guess I should have mentioned that," Rian said. "Our Wren, if you couldn't tell, is a prissy Nadre-ender. Ever heard of Cage Street? Yeah, I see the look on your faces. He lives there; this bastard is rich as shit, so don't feel bad about spending his money."

"Rian," Wren said. "If you tell literally anyone else where I live or who I am, then our friendship is over."

He watched enviously as Rian swallowed his wine, and then turned to Caspian when he noticed that he wasn't as enthusiastic about his drink. For a moment they stared at one another. Wren's eyes were so green, so kind-looking despite his abrasive personality.

Caspian drifted, listening more to the voice in his ears than anything else.

Frowning, Wren said, "Dominique, I'm borrowing your friend."

Without giving either of them the time to object or say anything otherwise, Wren grabbed Caspian by the arm and pulled him off the stall. His grip wasn't harsh or painful. On the contrary, Wren was gentle with him, carefully leading him out of the bar and onto Caulend's streets.

The sun had nearly set by now, and the evening, while still muggy, was cooler than before. Drunken men and women came and went as Wren led him around to the side of The Otherground where it was quiet, where they were alone. Everything felt mildly askew, as if Caspian was watching it all happen through a pair of eyes that weren't his own.

"Hey," Wren said, his voice low. "You, Caspian, look at me."

Caspian *was* looking at him. His breath came quickly, but he didn't know how to slow it down. The temperature dropped further, further, until Caspian could see each panicked exhale visible in the air.

Wren shivered. "Don't like wine? Don't think that's worth getting arrested over. You know you're violating a couple hundred laws right now, right?"

Wine? Oh. Wine. What Wren had bought them. Shaking his head, Caspian said, "It wasn't the drink."

"You're not giving me much to work with here," Wren said, his eyes flitting back and forth. He seemed unsure, though of what exactly, Caspian didn't know. "That Dominique woman, is she your girlfriend?"

Easy question. Difficult answer. "We're not together."

Wren ran a hand through his own hair. "But you do love her, don't you?"

"I don't like labels."

"Who does? Hah...love, it's weird, isn't it? I don't put much stock in it, personally. Relationships, all that, life's easier without them."

Caspian didn't know what to say. Wren's tangent was difficult to untangle. "You wouldn't ever want to be with someone?"

"Why would I put myself through that kind of grief?" He rubbed at

43

his face, wincing as he pushed hard against the bruised side. "Ow, damn. Forgot about that. How bad does it look?"

"Uh." There seemed to be no rhyme or reason to the questions that Wren was asking. He'd dragged him out here, but for what? "I can't lie to you, it looks messy. I've seen that sort of bruising before, that guy must have hit you hard."

"You're telling me! Great, thanks for the honesty, though. Can you believe that Empathra punched me? The gall of it. He started it anyway, asking me where I was from. I guess he took note of my clothes, my mistake, I don't usually come around here dressed so well, but Rian caught me off guard today asking me to go around and help him with that information. Anyway, so the Empathra asks me where I'm from, so I say, hey, don't you remember me?"

"You knew him?"

"I told him that I was a client of his from Risthe-end, buying his magic to work through my grief after my partner was killed in a recent boating accident, and how could he not recognize me? He just stared at me after I told him that I'd taken up a new career as a travelling merchant, though. Turns out he wasn't interested in my wares."

He pulled a notebook from his bag, shoving it into Caspian's hands. It was as generic as they came, but when he flipped through the first couple of pages, he found it filled with elegant script.

"What *is* this?" Caspian asked, unable to read the handwriting immediately.

"Old scriptures about a hidden split in Nadre-end," Wren said. "Constra! The most sacred of magic, light and stars and wishes. The stuff of dreams, the magic of Seldist, an entire continent away."

Caspian was about to ask where he'd happened upon such a thing, but then he flipped to a nearly blank page that had only one thing written on it. It took him a second to decipher the handwriting, but when he did, the entire charade fell apart.

Put through that application!

"Oh," Caspian said, somewhat disheartened. "You're lying, aren't you?"

Wren shrugged. "That's what the Empathra said. And when I told him that he was an idiot, he lost his temper. Now my parents are going to have my head."

Caspian was starting to see exactly why the Empathra had punched him. Returning the notebook to Wren, he said, "I'm sorry for asking, but what was the point in this? Did you just want me to tell you to put your application through?"

"No, I'm going to do that myself. Did it help?"

"Did what help? Reading your planner? No. Your handwriting is awful, I couldn't make anything out."

"But my handwriting is perfect," Wren said, sounding genuinely confused. "That wasn't what I meant anyway. Can you hear your water anymore?"

The question caught him off guard. No normal person had ever asked him that before. When he considered it, he realised he couldn't; his breathing had returned to normal. "I can't. You did this to distract me? To help me out?"

"I did it because I was bored." Wren walked past him. Caspian turned, trying to see his expression, but he kept his back turned to him. "That's why I do anything at all, really. Ilia, they suffer with their magic from time to time, and when I saw you looking out of it in there, I figured that might be the issue. Sorry I made you freak out, I only said that stuff about spreading your name because I thought you'd get a bit jumpy, not because I thought it'd send you spiralling. My mistake, I shouldn't have done it."

"It's alright," Caspian said. "I'm just surprised you even knew about that kind of thing."

"Yeah, well, that's that. Anyway, I'm going to tell Rian I need to head off. I wasn't joking about my parents, they're strict, you see, and they're going to give me an earful for turning up looking like this. So, coming with, or are you going to spend the rest of the night back here?"

He left before Caspian could answer. Instead of chasing him, he stood there a moment longer, contemplating the situation. Wren

Sharp was an oddity, one he couldn't figure out. Whatever was going on his head, Caspian couldn't understand him.

He didn't have the energy to try, either. Something was happening in Aquiline, and he and Dominique had to figure out what they would do next. It couldn't be Ezra at the centre of their issues, he knew that because he was dead, and yet he couldn't shake the feeling.

What if it was?

This would not end quietly. Caspian knew as much already.

CHAPTER 6

IN SOME OF DOMINIQUE'S FONDEST MEMORIES, EZRA PURNELL HAD been kind.

She'd known him for most of her life, since they'd both been just old enough to set fire to sticks with their fledgling flames. She'd always been an adventurous girl, outspoken and fearless. He'd been the same, and perhaps that was where their problems had begun.

There was a saying in Aquiline; *those with power become their power.* Normal folk didn't seem to realise just how true it was, but Dominique had seen it time and time again. There wasn't much variety in Ilia living in the city, but she'd never met a meek fire Elementra, nor had she ever encountered a bold water one. She'd never known earth or lightning based Ilia well enough to make a judgement, but when she considered it, she'd never met an out of touch Empathra either.

Personalities differed as they always did, but when it came to Ilia, there were certain core traits that came up consistently. Ezra had been fire through and through, burning brilliantly until he'd become destructive. They'd played as children and she'd fallen for that very fire as they'd grown into adults. It had been him, not her, who Caspian had been drawn in by when they'd welcomed him into their circle later.

Three days after she and Caspian had met with Wren and Rian, Dominique went back to Mellingdale. It was still early morning when she made the walk, but the sun was already high, the heat unpleasant even to her. Caspian had managed to find some work sharpening blades for a merchant for the day, so she was on her own. For the best, she thought; if he knew what she was up to, he'd have no doubt already tried to talk her out of it.

When she arrived, she set to work, approaching the early morning crowds in search of the same information Rian had found. There were a few faces that she recognized from when she'd lived there, and many of them recognized her back. That wasn't to say they were of any help; Rian had been right when he said people got shifty regarding her. Many wouldn't even meet her eyes.

One failure after another, the people she didn't know personally outright ignored her when they spotted her bracelet. It felt like she was being watched, eyes on her from every corner, but when she turned to meet them head-on, every gaze was directed at the floor. It was likely the remaining Ilpol making her nervous, but telling herself that didn't help.

Eventually she gave up, heading to the market street to grab something cheap for breakfast. The currant buns smelled the best, homely and inviting, but when she joined the queue, she found another Ilpol officer ahead of her, a tall woman with wavy brown hair that reached her waist. For a moment, Dominique considered going to a different stall, but nothing else appealed. She simply had to resign herself to the wait.

Nervously, she bounced from foot to foot as she waited her turn. Though she knew she'd done nothing wrong, she couldn't help it. The transaction ahead of her went faster than she anticipated, and just as Dominique decided to try and cross her arms to hide the bracelet, the officer turned around.

A pause. Her eyes widened a fraction. "Oh! Excuse me, you're an Elementra with an affinity for fire?"

"I am," Dominique said stiffly, stepping past her so that she could get her own bun.

"Do you mind if I—"

48

"Am I a suspect?"

"No."

"Then yes, I do mind," Dominique selected a bun and traded a couple of coins for it. She shoved it into her mouth more for the opportunity to not have to speak than the flavour.

She was about to leave when the officer spoke again, softer this time. "Please, just give me a second. I don't mean to intrude, I don't even wish to keep you. I just wondered if you might know anything about what happened here?"

Dominique considered telling her to scarper, but she had the reputation of the Ilia to consider. Stepping to the side so the next customer could get to the stall, she took another bite of her bun. "Look, I'm in the same position as you. I don't know anything, but I wish I did. Then I could actually figure out what's going on in this forsaken district."

The woman looked a little surprised, but she nodded nonetheless. "Understandable. My name is Erica Robertson, I'm an officer with the Ilpolitia. My partner went missing the other night while patrolling Mellingdale, and all we've managed to recover is his badge. His name is Aidan, did you maybe see him?"

"I don't live here, so no. I'm from Caul-end." Dominique finished the bun and brushed the crumbs from her fingers. "I did come here on the night of the fire, but that was to help put it out. I'm actually looking for who started it, do you know anything?"

Erica shook her head, looking forlornly at her own bun, which she had yet to start. "It seems we're at a stalemate. We've had prior reports from here about an Elementra, but the name they kept giving us was that of a dead man. I might have to start considering it, but nobody will tell me anything now. I don't think the people trust us."

It was hardly a surprise given the Ilpol's reputation, but Dominique didn't mention that. Instead, she considered the information. It made enough sense, even if Caspian didn't want to believe it. Six months. It was long enough to recover. Long enough to get affairs in order.

"Did you find anything else—" Dominique began, only for a scream to split the air, cutting off her question. Both she and Erica snapped their heads around, but it didn't seem to be in their immediate vicinity.

"Fire!" a woman's voice shrieked. "Another fire!"

It was nearby. People began moving, rushing, looking at one another in shock and surprise. Erica set off immediately in the direction the voice had come from, and Dominique didn't hesitate to follow. The two of them sprinted, Erica taking her to an alleyway where a woman stood, screaming and pointing. "Someone's burning! They're burning!"

The fire was not like the one from the previous night, far smaller, actually contained. Piles of rubbish were alight, and like the woman had cried, there was a body amidst the flames. Erica darted forwards, tearing off her standard-issue waistcoat in an attempt to smother the fire. Dominique went after her, already trying to manipulate the flames, trying to quell them.

But it wasn't working. They stubbornly refused to bend to her will, fighting back against her interference, intensifying in the face of it. "Not natural," she breathed, trying harder. Still no success. "These flames are the work of an Elementra!"

"Jaime!" Erica cried, desperately trying to force the fire out through her own means. "Someone, get me water! Help me!"

Dominique looked further up the alleyway. Whoever had done this, if it had been Ezra, then he'd been here not long ago. She set off running, leaving the fire and Erica behind. She had to find him—if it *was* him, then he was their best chance of putting it out.

"Ezra!" she called out. "Ezra, if it's you...!"

There was nowhere in Ardr-end that he used to frequent, nowhere that she was certain he would be. If Erica had known the person burning in the alley, it was likely that they were Ilpol, and if he'd felt the need to lash out, then it meant he'd been cornered, his back against the wall. He *had* to be close.

"Ezra!" she shouted again. "I know you're there!"

She bashed past people who stared after her. She didn't care. He was alive, she knew it now, and she had to find him. She had to find him before—

Before what?

He killed again? Burned again? She didn't know, she just had to see him. She pushed through the panicked groups, turning down backstreets, the places where few people ventured in the day. The one person she knew she should never want to see again, and here she was, desperate to see his face.

The smell of smoke hit her like she'd run into a brick wall. She stopped in her tracks, spotting someone ahead, someone hidden between the dingy, darkened buildings. Ardr-end's backstreets were like Caul-end's, cramped and tight, utterly claustrophobic. Even during the day there was very little light to see with, but that only made the man before her stand out more. He had a flame burning at his fingertips, bright and bold, shadows dancing on his face.

Dominique held her breath as he turned to her. She could feel her heartbeat, rattling her ribcage with every pulse. The fire screamed endlessly in her veins. *Burn it down.*

He put the flame out and walked towards her. Despite summer's approach, despite her own power, the space between them was like ice. They stared at one another, his gaze so intense that she feared it would burn a hole through her.

Shaven hair, eyes so red that they might as well have been on fire. His skin was utterly ruined with scarring, and his handsome features had been destroyed, the traits of an Ilia too powerful for his own good. She'd dreamt this moment before, but he'd not looked like this at all. In her imagination, he'd been beautiful and whole and terrifying; Ezra as he'd been, not the shadow that stood before her now.

"I knew you'd figure out it was me. I knew you'd chase me," he said, and before she could make her voice work, he grabbed her.

She tensed, but it was just a hug. Against his chest, it was unbearable, too warm, too tight, too dangerous. She'd convinced herself that she'd prepared herself for this, but now, up close, she wondered if chasing him had been a mistake.

"I knew you'd come back to me," he said. Her magic buzzed in her ears, nearly drowning out his voice. "I've been looking for you, and Caspy too. Where is he?"

"He couldn't be here," Dominique said, her voice clipped. There was no way to escape his hold. All she could do was ride it out, do her best not to upset him until she could put some distance between them. "How are you alive? We thought you were dead."

She felt the laugh vibrate in his chest. "I don't just 'die', Domi. I thought I'd killed you, though, you and Caspy…but you both escaped, huh? You got out. I'm so proud."

He pushed her back gently, both hands on her shoulders. She'd wanted this. She'd wanted to see him again, but now she could remember every single instance of him raising his voice, or his hand, his temper igniting like flame to gasoline.

"That person in the alley, why did you hurt them?" She fought to keep her voice steady. "It was you, wasn't it? You might have killed them."

"Don't matter, does it? I was gonna call you out with a little fire, but she saw and came for me. I just stopped her in her tracks. Weren't my fault that she got aggressive, right?"

She shook her head, stepping back. The space between them didn't make her feel any better; she could feel the sweat on her forehead. "You burned down Mellingdale too. I thought I wanted to see you, I was hoping you were alive, but you did all that…you've killed, Ezra. Why?"

"You know why," Ezra said. Dominique's stomach twisted. "Had to make an impression so you noticed, and I had to do something so the magic would stop shouting. It's so loud, Domi. I hear it constantly. Burn it all. Burn it all. Burn it all."

"That's no excuse," Dominique said, hoping that she could get through to him. Sometimes, she'd been able to talk him down. "I hear it too, and I'm not setting everything on fire. Do you think I'll be sympathetic? I won't. You have to stop this."

He looked at her, eyebrows drawing together. "What?"

"You heard me. You can't keep doing this."

His confused expression told her that he genuinely didn't under-stand. "Domi, listen to me, that's not…don't you *want* to see it burn? All three of us together, watching everything fall, don't you want that?"

Not it was her turn to be confused. Not a single word out of his mouth made sense. "What are you saying?"

When he grabbed her by the shoulder again, his fingers were warm. She felt them through the fabric of her shirt. "I want to torch this city, I want to see it *burn*. That's why I've been looking for you, we'll do it together, the three of us. Where are you living now? Take me back there. Need to make sure Caspy's okay too, after all. You know what he's like."

Her own skin burned, her fear making her boil. He sounded insane. "You can't burn the city down! That's ridiculous!"

"Is it?" He tightened his grip. "Don't you want to see it? The blaze, the flames, how hot they'll burn. Take me back to your place, Domi. I need to say sorry to Caspy for what happened. He'll forgive me if I go to him, the same way you've forgiven me by coming here."

"Forgiven you?" She choked on the words. "You're not forgiven. You really think that you can do this? That you can go out there and burn it all and that I'll *forgive* you? You don't get that luxury! You don't even get—!"

His fingers seared through her shirt. She tore herself from his grasp, turning her back on him as she bit back the cry in her throat. Though she was resistant to burns, that didn't mean she was immune.

"Shit," Ezra stepped back from her, his voice higher-pitched than before. "Domi, just shut up. I didn't mean that, you know I didn't. Just…just shut up. Stop talking."

You know I didn't mean it. Just like that, she knew that nothing had changed, that all of her dreams could never come true. She'd let him mistreat them again and again because of that one line, because she'd believed it.

It had always been out of his control, he said. He never *really* meant to hurt them, but he still did, time and time again.

"No," she said. "You don't get to say that to me."

She heard him shift behind her. "Stop this, Domi. I missed you. You know that, right? I love you."

No, you don't, she thought.

He touched her again, one hand on her upper arm. She twisted and shoved him hard in the chest with burning hands. He tried to grab her, but he hadn't expected her to fight and missed entirely, his hands grabbing at nothing as he fell back hard into a nearby wall. "Domi!"

She ran back the way she came, not once looking back to see if he was coming after her. She knew him well enough to know he would give chase. All she could do was put distance between them and try to find somewhere crowded, somewhere where he wouldn't be able to show his face.

Erica. Dominique rushed back towards the alleyway where the burning woman had been found, and then past it once she saw the crowd. The Ilpol would stop her if they saw her, and though she would be safer with them than with Ezra, it was too much of a risk to take. She didn't stop at the station either, running on until her lungs burned and her chest ached, pain ricocheting through her sides from the strain.

It had been her mistake. She'd been the one who'd been too curious. If Ezra came after her, if he found their home and hurt either her or Caspian, it was on her head for poking the hornet's nest.

If she didn't lose him now, the last six months they'd spent rebuilding their lives would have been for nothing.

Dominique burst into The Otherground in such a panic that two people near the entrance nearly fell from their seats in surprise. Several others whirled around on their stalls to investigate the commotion for themselves. It was the perfect place, still busy despite the earlier hour, and full of prying eyes. She'd chosen it specifically because it wasn't home. If Ezra was still tailing her, then at least he wouldn't find their safe haven.

Cami was there, standing steadfast behind the bar. Their eyes met, and Dominique rushed over, planting her hands on the counter to steady herself. Her entire body felt numb. Her chest was too tight.

"Hey, firecracker," Cami said, sounding concerned. "You okay?"

Dominique chanced a look behind her. Ezra wasn't there. "I did something stupid."

"What?"

Her magic hummed an angry song in her veins. When she spoke

again, the words were garbled. "I did something so stupid. I can't breathe."

She remained frozen there until Cami came out and guided her onto a stall. "Sit down, sweetheart. Do you need help? I've got an Empathra in here today, we could ask her for help. Their type can remove negative emotions for a price."

Dominique shook her head. If she'd wanted an Empathra, she'd have asked for one.

"Yeesh, bunch of prying bastards, huh?" sang a different voice, one Dominique was familiar with, but couldn't place. "Oi! Nothing to see here, everyone turn those pretty little heads around and get back to drinking!"

She stared down at her hands, flames licking at her fingertips. The magic hissed, *burn it down.*

"Burn what down?" she asked.

All of it.

"Hey, sweetheart," Cami said. When Dominique looked up, she saw her stood there, toying with the bronze stone she wore around her neck. "No magic here, remember?"

"Can't help it," Dominique said. Her cheeks were wet. She hadn't even realised she'd been crying.

"Proper fire that is," the other voice said. Dominique dashed a hand across her eyes and looked over, only to find Rian McCarrick sat in the same stall as the previous night. Wren wasn't at his side this time. "You might wanna be careful, lass. You might start something."

"I won't," she said, but even to herself, she didn't sound certain. "Are you always here?"

"Nah, but my dad kicked me out the house and told me to enjoy myself." Rian scowled as he said it, the first time she'd seen him look anything other than pleased. "Stupid bastard, can barely breathe 'cause his lungs are so bad, but wants me to get out and do something. Can't say no to him, see, even though I've got no cash to blow on anything. So, what about you? Are *you* always here?"

"Don't be snide," Cami cut in, giving him a look. "Ignore him, Domi. What do you mean when you say that you made a mistake?"

She found it difficult to answer. All she could think of was fire, of

Ezra and his heat. He was meant to be dead, they were supposed to be safe. It was meant to be their happy ending, but now it was anything but.

"I went looking for something I shouldn't have," she said after a moment, her eyes stinging as she tried to hold back the tears. "I've ruined it all."

Cami bit her lip. Dominique couldn't bear her pitiful expression. She didn't want the sympathy; it had been her mistake, her own fault. She'd made the decision to seek out the truth, and now she had to live with it.

"Question! Would you change it if you could?" asked Rian. Cami shot him a look, which he returned in kind. "What? I'm just asking her what you'd ask me, or any other poor sap who decides to unload their personal bullshit on you."

"Rian!"

Rian protested his case, but Dominique barely heard it. She thought back to earlier that morning when she'd been lying in bed, agonising over whether or not Ezra was still around. If she'd done nothing, she'd still be there, still wondering, still tearing herself apart.

"Why would you ask me that?" she said.

"Cami does it all the time. I thought I'd give it a try. I mean, think about it this way; everything's gonna end sometime, right? That's the way life goes. We live, we breathe, we die, no point in worrying about it. So, here's the question she asks: if you managed to figure out how your story's gonna end, would it change what you did? Would you try to fix the ending if you hated it, or would you just accept whatever came to pass?"

His brown eyes were bright as he spoke, his tone passionate. She listened closely, trying to envision a version of herself that wasn't obsessed with her own power, that had a better grip on her abilities. Maybe if she'd never met Ezra, if she'd never let him influence her, she'd be that person.

Would she change that meeting then?

No. There was no point in it. If not Ezra, someone else would have waltzed into her life and warped her to their liking. Ezra Purnell had always been poison in her veins, but she couldn't deny that she'd been injecting him daily. Love was a powerful thing. Like the way her fire killed her every time she used it, like the way cigarette smoke blackened the lungs of the smoker, her love for him had been a slow death. The misery of staying with him had been one more thing that she'd been addicted to, and if she'd never met him, she'd never have met Caspian either.

That was her answer, as unfortunate as it was. It was her truth, as much as she hated it. "I wouldn't change a thing. For better or for worse, what I've been through shaped me into the person I am."

"Good answer. I agree lass." Rian looked smug as he said it. "Wren bloody hates that way of thinking, he does, but I believe that whatever happens is the way things *should* be. Hey! Check me out, Cami, I'm doing your job for you. Hire me?"

"Unlikely, McCarrick," Cami said, giving Dominique another concerned glance. "He didn't upset you with that spiel, did he? I only ask people that question when it's appropriate, and right now *wasn't*."

"Bull," Rian said delightedly. "I've seen you pull that question on people having straight breakdowns, I have."

Dominique couldn't care less for who Cami did or didn't question. All she knew was that her heart had calmed a little in her chest, and her tears had dried. Two almost-strangers, and yet she felt so much better around them. Was it a sign? Were they worth trusting wholly?

Burn it down, said her power. She winced. "Thanks for the advice, really, but I need to go."

She stood, only for Rian to call out to her. "Nah, what's the rush? Stay a little while, lass. Take a drink. The world ain't going anywhere, and you look like you could do with it."

Dominique hesitated, but Cami gave her an encouraging nod. "This place is safe, and I do my best to keep the patrons on the straight and narrow. Feel free to hang around. McCarrick will keep you company no matter what, so be prepared to have your ear talked off if you do stay."

The kindness was almost too much to bear. "Why do you care so much? You both barely know me."

Cami's hand went to the stone at her neck, her fingers stroking its smooth surface. "Sometimes, honey, you see someone who you think needs help. Right now, I think that's you. My job would be a lot more depressing if I didn't offer a few kind words now and then, that's for sure."

"And as for me, you're interesting, and I like interesting people." Rian gestured to the stall next to him, an invitation to sit. "Know what my dad said when I told him about you guys? He went, 'Rian, my lad, you're gonna end up falling so far in with them Ilia that you're gonna go and get yourself some powers in a split before long!' I laughed at him for it, but, you know what? I think I'm more invested in your little story than ever now."

Interested. In her. Dominque shook her head, a laugh escaping her throat. "You mean that, don't you?"

"We do. So, you gonna stay, lass?"

The answer should have been yes, but her magic refused to give her peace. She had to figure out her next move fast, figure out how to get ahead of Ezra before he could find them again. "I appreciate it, I really do, but I can't. I have somewhere to be."

Disappointment crossed both Cami and Rian's faces, but Dominique had no choice. Her magic still screeched. Her fingers itched with the urge to burn. It wasn't safe to stay, not when she was so dangerous.

"Wait," Cami began.

Dominique turned to leave. "I'm sorry, but I have to go."

CHAPTER 7

CASPIAN RETURNED TO AN EMPTY HOUSE.

He tried to pay it no mind as he went inside. It wasn't strange for Dominique to go out during the day; she'd likely just gone to try and secure a job for tomorrow, or maybe just for a breath of fresh air. It should have been a simple explanation, but he'd seen her earlier that morning before he'd left, how she'd been on edge and flighty, staring at the ceiling and barely responding to his questions. She hadn't been present, not truly, and that was where his worries stemmed from.

He couldn't help but fear for her when she was like that, because he knew first-hand how easy it was so slip on magic when it was influenced by emotion. But there was nothing he could do, not when he didn't know where she'd gone, so he simply dropped the cash he'd earned into the pot they shared and went to wait by the windowsill.

It hadn't been legal work today. He'd helped a blacksmith by using his power to cool the iron, but he'd only managed to snag the job through happenstance and luck alone. Without a license, it was punishable by the law to use his magic for most anything, but the blacksmith had been desperate, and Caspian had thing one thing that many other water-based Elementras lacked. He could control ice with near perfect precision when he really put his mind to it.

It had been manageable at the time, but now the work was done and his body hated him for it. He sat on the windowsill, his back against the frame, and stared out over the city as he tried not to fall asleep. It looked so different from this view, smoggy and ill. Perhaps Aquiline would one day choke to death on itself. It would hardly be a surprise if it did.

He was dozing when the noise of the door clicking shut made him jump. Groggily, he sat up straight, turning his head as Dominque called out, "Caspy?"

"I'm here," he said. When she walked into the room, his heart sank; her face was stone, her fists clenched. In an instant, he was wide awake, concern pushing him to his feet. "I got back a while ago, but you weren't here. Is everything okay?"

He waited, but she didn't answer, her gaze finding the floor. Something was wrong. "Domi?"

He stepped forward. She met him there, throwing her arms around him, a crushing hug. Freezing in her gasp, he felt the heat of her fingers even through the fabric of his shirt. His tired magic twisted in response. Though he knew he wasn't in danger, he didn't feel safe.

"I did something stupid, Caspian," Dominique said, breathy and broken. "Ezra's still alive."

Caspian didn't realise how far he'd dropped the temperature in the room until Dominique stepped back from him, her breath visible as she hugged herself. He shook his head. "No. You're wrong."

"I spoke to him," Dominique said, shivering. "He attacked an Ilpol officer in Ardr-end today, and it was him who burned down Mellingdale. He's alive, and he hasn't changed, Caspian. He wants us to go back to him and I don't know what to do!"

In his blood, it was a desperate fight for control. He had to get a grip on himself and return the temperature to normal. "Does he know where we are?"

"No."

"Did he hurt you?"

"I ran, went to The Otherground. Rian and Cami helped me out."

It was a relief, but it still didn't settle him. He slumped against the windowsill, his energy drained. What could he do? How could they move forward now?

"Why did you do it?" he asked. "Why did you have to go looking for him? Why couldn't you just let it be?"

"I know I shouldn't have, but I had to know." Dominique still couldn't meet his eyes. "He set that fire for us, Caspian. He wanted to send us the message that he was looking. When he realised I didn't have you with me, he got angry. He wants us both."

"If he's in the city, we can't stay here. We need to leave. Aquiline's too dangerous now!"

"No." Anger flashed across her features. The magic in her pupils was stark red. "Running again? We're always running! We could protect ourselves if he came for us, we'd just need to work together!" She stepped forward, gripping him by the shoulders. "We have that kind of power. We could do it!"

In the light of the setting sun, she looked manic, unlike herself. Her hands left burning impressions. "We can't fight him, Dominique!"

"If he doesn't come after us, we won't have to! Anything that happens to him would be his own fault!" Her hold grew tighter as her voice rose, and Caspian's magic rose in turn, trying to counteract the heat. "He *will* come, Caspian, he wants things to go back to how they were, but we can't let it happen!"

"Going up against him will only end badly, you know that!"

"Not if we're stronger than him!"

"We're *out of control!* Your hands are blazing!"

She recoiled instantly, looking down at her hands in horror. Silence hung between them like a guillotine, only her words dropping the blade. "Caspian, no, no, I'm so sorry."

She hadn't hurt him. Unlike Ezra, she hadn't intended to do him damage. "Enough of this, Dominique. We're not fighting our way out of this because we can't. It isn't just Ezra we have to worry about, it's ourselves. If we hurt or kill someone, even another Ilia, the Ilpol won't overlook it!"

Dominique pulled her hands close to her chest. "I hadn't...I hadn't thought about that..."

It wasn't just that, either. It was their own health they had to be concerned with. "We'll be okay. We just need to think this through."

"Maybe we should just stick with your plan then. Forget what I said, we can just try and save our money and then get out of here. He doesn't know where we live, I made sure of it, so…as long as we avoid Ardr-end, he shouldn't find us."

She didn't sound certain, but as far as Caspian could see, it was their only option. They could hope for a miracle, that the Ilpol would deal with Ezra themselves, but even if they went to them now, what information could they offer them? They didn't know Ezra's whereabouts, or what his next move would be. It was useless.

Dominique wrapped her arms around herself again, making herself small. Caspian stopped himself from reaching out to her. Unless she initiated contact, he didn't touch her, because Ezra had only ever grabbed and grabbed. He knew for himself the kind of scars that left.

"We'll be okay," he said, hoping the words didn't sound as hollow as they felt. "Dominique?"

She looked at him, and then she reached out of her own accord. She ghosted her hand over the right side of his chest, where, beneath his shirt, his skin was discoloured and uneven. "I would never hurt you like that, Caspian. I swear it."

The scarring there was Ezra's final gift, the reason why Dominique had fought back for that day six months ago, the direct precursor to the fire that had torn apart their home. Ezra had left his mark, and it had been no accident, it had been the first time Caspian had felt like he couldn't blame himself for Ezra's fury. It had been the first time he'd felt rage back.

"Forget him and what he did," Caspian pleaded. "It's just me and you now, just us."

And perhaps, in a better world where Ezra did not exist, he would have kissed her then, but they were both too damaged for something like that. He'd never told her about how he felt, not when there were too many words and they were both still trying to heal. One day, maybe, but not then.

62

Not when everything was still so raw.

"We'll make it, right?" Dominique said, stepping back.

Caspian nodded. Ezra didn't know where they were. They still had time.

CHAPTER 8

THOUGH EZRA HAD TRAWLED THE STREETS OF CAUL-END ALL afternoon searching for any hint of Dominique, it looked like she was long gone.

Once again she'd slipped from his grasp, shouting at him all the while that he'd been in the wrong when it simply wasn't true. That look in her eyes, the way she'd thought it okay to attack him, why hadn't she understood? Couldn't she hear her magic the way he did? Its mad mutterings were his eternal companion, constantly screeching in his ears.

It wasn't that he wanted to burn everything, it was that he *had* to. Nothing else would make the voice shut up quite like a display of fire and brimstone.

He thought of her again, how beautiful she'd been even with that look of hatred on her face. How he'd missed them, Dominique and Caspian both. They were the two people that he'd give anything for, the only two people that he wanted at his side when he scorched everything in his path, but Caspian hadn't even bothered to come with Dominique to find him. He hadn't even tried.

The thought boiled his blood, because, at first, he'd thought that he'd killed them. In the days after the fire, before the papers began reporting that he was the only one who'd lost his life, he'd tortured himself over and over with the realisation that he'd lost them to his own power. He'd spent every waking moment since his recovery trying to find them, he'd put every second to use, and apparently, neither Dominique nor Caspian had even bothered looking for him in turn. The state of Caul-end only stoked his fury. It was a mess of a district that they'd taken up residence in, not at all what either of them deserved.

He was going to take them out of the city when everything was over, find a place that was quiet and isolated, and then it would be the three of them together again. Just like it was meant to be.

As he searched a street that stank of piss and vomit, his magic spiked within him, sending ripples of pain through his chest. He staggered, grabbing a nearby wall for support. Rot. It felt like rot, a sensation he was no stranger to. His organs were turning to dust, decaying from the inside.

Burn it all. Burn it all. Those were the words he heard, the compulsion in his head. How badly he wanted to listen. How badly he needed to obey.

"Excuse me, Sir?" Ezra turned his head to find a young man behind him, the badge of an Ilpol inspector displayed on his shirt. He had a stern face and a lean build; the only thing out of place on him was his hat, which sat slightly askew on his head. "Are you alright?"

Ezra gave a breathy laugh. How careless of him, letting an Ilpol follow him unnoticed. "Do I look alright? Screw you. Leave me alone."

The inspector didn't even blink. "I'm afraid I can't do that, Sir. You happen to match the description of someone I've been told to be on the lookout for, so do you mind if I ask you a couple of questions?"

"Rude, ain't it, asking me that? You go up to every Ilia and ask if they're a criminal?"

"Of course not. I endeavour to treat everyone with respect, Ilia or not. That being said, I cannot simply ignore you now. May I ask your name?"

Ezra scowled. This Ilpol was better than the last two he'd encountered, impartial, not too aggressive with his line of questioning. "I don't have to tell you *shit*."

Despite his rising tone, the inspector stood his ground, entirely unfazed. "Two of Ardr-end's assigned officers have been found dead in recent days, so forgive my impatience, but this matter is serious. Are you Ezra Purnell?"

Ezra grabbed the man by his shirt and slammed him against the same wall that he'd been previously leaning against. A few people around them gasped. Someone shouted. His power burned in his chest like a furnace, the rot spreading further. This was who he was, flame given form.

"So what if I am?" he asked, his voice low. "Splits, I hate you damn Ilpol, sticking your nose into my business constantly. I'm giving you the chance I didn't give them, get out of here and leave me be. You'll do it if you know what's good for you."

The inspector held his hands up. He didn't look frightened, not like the others when they realised who he was. "Please calm down. I see that you're having difficulty containing your magic. If you can't control yourself, that won't help your case."

No cell would ever contain him. Even if the inspector did take him in, Ezra was no weakling ember, he was a wildfire that refused to be tamed. "You ain't the first to spot me," he said, having made up his mind about the man's fate. "I don't reckon you're gonna be the last either.

Finally, he saw something change in the inspector's expression, a brief moment of alarm that was so rich that the fire inside Ezra thrived. Some people had run off by now. Others had run to them, all watching—but this was Caul-end. Nobody would step in to help some Ilpol.

"Don't do something you'll regret," said the inspector, lowering his hands to where his baton was. How valiant. He wasn't going to beg or plead? The second one had done that, the woman, she'd cried for him to stop.

Magic was easy to use. All it took was a thought, an intention, and his hand lit up in flames. The inspector reacted, smashing his head forwards into Ezra's. The unexpected blow sent him reeling back, the fire going out, his magic hissing in questioning tones.

The inspector grabbed him by his wrists, using his surprise against him. Yanking them around behind him, he reached for his handcuffs.

Ezra snarled, heating his skin, but the inspector was better than he had initially given him credit for, not letting go in the slightest. There was nothing for it then. Ezra set his own skin alight, the inspector jumping back with an alarmed shout. The people around them grew loud, but they were nothing more than a distraction to be ignored.

The Ilpolitia were useless as a force when an Ilia went all out against them; it was what they got for only employing regular folk, for being so scared of magic. They had no *idea* what they were truly up against.

His skin still on fire, Ezra turned, grabbing the inspector by his shirt anew. The damage he'd done himself physically wasn't so bad, thanks to his resistance. It was that very power that had saved him in the fire of six months ago—but that didn't mean it was painless. The raging agony of his self-immolation made him slower to react, and the inspector was quick. His baton smashed into his forehead, and, dizzied, Ezra dropped him. He felt blood, his skin split by the blow.

"You are under arrest," the inspector said. "Do not attempt to use force, or you will face the consequences."

Ezra laughed through the pain. Throwing his hand out, he let the flames leap from his fingertips. The inspector dashed right, trying to get out of his way, but Ezra had tired of the games. Left, right, forwards, he tossed his magic everywhere, pillars of furious flame growing, the inspector trapped between them.

Screaming. Shouting. The inspector looked at his impossible situation, and then back to Ezra. "If you kill me, the Ilpolitia will not let this go. Know that."

"Who are you kidding? They can't stop me." Ezra closed in on him again, only for him to swing that blasted baton at him again. He grabbed it with his burning hands, fighting against the pain as he snatched it from his grip. The inspector had no time to defend himself as Ezra struck back, smashing it into the side of his head.

It worked as intended, the inspector staggering back from the blow, his hat falling from the force. Ezra tossed the baton to the flames and snatched him up by the throat, sneering in his face. He hadn't intended to kill any of the Ilpol, but they just kept getting in his way.

"You put up a better fight than the others, but here's a message for the Ilpol," he said. "If you weren't so incompetent, then maybe you'd figure out a way to stop me!"

His magic howled with delight as he let it loose, the flames consuming the both of them. The inspector screamed as Ezra threw him to the pillars, stepping back as he put out the fire that had caught on his skin. His clothes were charred, his skin burned, but despite it all, he turned and ran.

People parted for him, their shouts mere background noise. Aftershocks built up within him, a spiralling inferno in his chest that tore through his lungs and spurred his heart into a frenzy. Damn his weakness. Damn his magic. Damn the world for making him so powerful, only to ruin him from the inside out.

He collapsed a little way off from a busy, run-down pub, his knees hitting the ground hard, his breaths ragged and choked. Another Ilpol added to the pile of bodies he was leaving behind, and it had cost him. The price of power was his very life. Every time he burned something, he paid for it with his time.

He spat on the ground at the injustice of it all. It was unfair. His entire life had been unfair. Ilia got nothing in Aquiline. Time and time again, he'd had his control ripped from him for reasons that he had no power over. Screw the Ilpol, who enforced their ugly rules. Screw the citizens who knew nothing about the struggles he'd faced. Screw Dominique and Caspian, who thought they could make their own way without them. He wanted them back so badly, but for what?

It had been them who had betrayed *him*. They'd been the ones to leave him behind.

"You alright there, mate?"

Ezra snapped his head up, wary of any other Ilpol who might have followed him, but it was just some scraggy-looking Ilia with dark brown hair and a matching bracelet. It was difficult to tell if he was tainted, or if it was just his natural colouring. Ezra's own grew in red tones nowadays when he didn't shave it off. Dominique's hair, he'd noticed, was redder than ever too.

She was succumbing to their addiction. She *had* to know how he felt.

"You know how it is," Ezra rasped.

"Yeah, I do," the Ilia nodded. "But you look like shit. Splits above, the amount of bloody fire Elementras you see around here that look proper mucked up. Saw one 'ere earlier who looked a right wreck. See 'em everywhere."

Ezra straightened up. "Short hair, a skinny thing, right? Was that who you saw? A woman?"

"Yeah."

"Did she have a guy with her? A water Elementra?"

The Ilia shook his head. "No guy with her. Why? You know her?"

"She's someone important to me. I need to find her."

The Ilia laughed. "Aw, I see how it is. Well, I don't know nothing else, but this bar might be a good place to start. Seen her a few times here this week, so I figure she's a regular or something. Ask around, 'cause I ain't got nothing else."

He'd already spent months asking around the entirety of Ardr-end. The idea of having to do another round of questioning hardly seemed appealing, but Ezra would do anything to find Dominique and Caspian. The other Ilia offered him a hand, which he gladly took.

Inside his power screamed anew, but now wasn't the time to listen. He had to focus on finding them, and only once they were together, could he rest.

Not long now; he was certain of it.

CHAPTER 9

"D<small>ID YOU HEAR?" ASKED A WOMAN NEAR THE STALL</small> D<small>OMINIQUE WAS</small> stood at. "Another Ilpol got killed the other day! The head-inspector of Caul-end! That makes three this week alone!"

Three days. It had been that long since Dominique had met with Ezra, and three days since she and Caspian had made the decision to leave Aquiline. She'd spent the time walking up and down Nadre-end while Caspian did the same in Caul-end, the two of them searching for anywhere that would give them work. More than ever they needed every penny they could scrape together, but it was beginning to look as if no one needed her brand of help.

Again, and again, she was turned away.

Again, and again.

Again, and again.

"Sorry, Miss. We don't require anyone with *your* skill set," said the man working behind the market stall. Dominique muttered a thank you and moved on, ignoring the gossiping of the women. It was the same excuse she'd been hearing all day, in the exact same tone of voice each time. Nadre-end was home to Aquiline's richest, but at the same time, it was also filled with bigots who cared little for Ilia.

What didn't help was the head inspector's death that the women were discussing. He'd been burned to death in the same fashion as the two before him, and the continuous deaths were fostering uncertainty in the public. As she walked past, people looked at her with disgust, like they blamed her even though eyewitness reports had said it was a man. Dominique knew well enough that it was Ezra, but that didn't stop people judging her.

He was catching up to them. She'd hoped that she might be able to save time by looking for higher paying jobs, but it seemed that she was only wasting it instead. Nobody wanted to take her, not before, and especially not now. Ripping the bracelet off seemed like a good idea in passing, but her appearance would give her away even without it. She'd be *asking* for the Ilpol to come and arrest her at that point.

She was just about to give up on Nadre-end when she passed by a sign directing her to Cage Street. The name rang bells in her mind, and it took her a moment to remember that Rian had mentioned it; it was where Wren lived. He was arrogant and irritating, but he also had money, and Rian's chatter indicated that he haemorrhaged it whenever he went out. If he was that free with his cash, maybe he would have an errand or two for her to run?

It was a shot in the dark, but she had no pride left, and it was only another five or so minutes wasted if she went and checked. Boldly, she went down the street, her head held high. The only challenge was in figuring out which prestigious-looking door he lived behind. They all looked identical, with only differing front gardens to tell them apart.

There was an old, sweet-looking lady tending to a hedge in front of one of the houses, so Dominique decided that she would have to do. "Excuse me," she said, trying to mould her accent into something that sounded a little less common. "I'm looking for someone called Wren. Do you think you could point me in the right direction? I wasn't given an address."

The woman eyed her up and down, her trimmers stilling. "Looking for his parents so they'll help you? I doubt you'll have much luck, but just down there. Number 24."

She pointed it out and then went back to her trimming. Dominique thanked her and approached the house. Even if Wren turned her down, it wouldn't be much of a blow, not when she had nothing to lose. The path to the door was neatly lined in roses and ferns, well-looked after and cared for. His family obviously enjoyed the garden.

Steeling herself, she knocked on the door. Seconds passed, dragging past her, and for a moment, she thought no one was going to answer. Were they out? She wouldn't come back if they were. There would be no point in it.

But then the door opened, an older version of Wren appearing in front of her. His hair was the same shade of brown, streaked through with grey, and a pair of glasses sat high on his nose. He narrowed his green eyes behind them in a perfect imitation of his son's favoured scowl and said, "Yes?"

She hadn't counted on someone *other* than Wren opening the door, but it seemed like she'd encountered his father instead. Wincing, she said, "I'm looking for Wren. Is he here?"

Wren's father sighed irritably. "What's he done this time to get an Ilia on my doorstep? Is this to do with that bloody McCarrick boy? It is, isn't it?"

It wasn't, but if that was her only way in, then so be it. "Rian asked me to come find him, actually. Is he not here?"

"No, he's not. Looks like you've been roped in on the other half of their agreement, whatever it is. He left about fifteen minutes ago claiming that he needed to go to Risthe-end to help him with something, even though he *knows* we have a dinner reservation this afternoon. Did you come from there?"

"Yes," Dominique lied. "I didn't see him on the way, though."

"Well, you just missed him then. If you go to the station, you might still catch him, but I don't know. For the love of…if he hasn't left by now, I doubt he'll get back in time. That boy makes me want to tear my hair out sometimes." Wren's father went to turn his back, only to stop. "I can't believe I'm asking an Ilia this, but if you *do* see him, tell him to come home. I know he's concerned about McCarrick's father, but I've already told him that there's nothing to be done, that we can only make him comfortable."

She nodded wordlessly as he shut the door in her face. Though she'd only met Wren twice, it was easy to see where he'd inherited some of his more unpleasant traits from. If he was frustrating to deal with, then his father was only more so.

Not that it was worth dwelling on. If Wren did have anything for her to do, then she needed to catch up with him, and if not, she could just go home. She set off immediately, crossing her fingers that she'd find him.

~

Cage Street's nearest station was bustling with activity when Dominique arrived, though not a single person seemed to actually be going anywhere. Every traveller she passed seemed inexplicably angry as she dodged in and out of their way, scanning their faces in her search for Wren.

He wasn't difficult to find. She spotted him stood off to the side with one of the station's attendants. The bruise on his face had only half-healed, giving him a decidedly rough look that didn't match up with his image in the slightest. She was certain that his father had been delighted when he'd seen him sporting the injury.

"There's no trains running at *all?*" he said, running his hand through the short strands of his hair. The man he was accosting looked as if he was barely listening. "Can you at least tell me what's happened? I have somewhere to be!"

Whatever the attendant offered up as an explanation was clearly unsatisfactory, as Wren threw his hands up and stormed away. Surprised that he'd given up his argument so quickly, Dominique intercepted him, stepping out to block his path. "Hello, Kinglet."

Wren raised his eyebrows. "You again? What are you doing in Nadre-end?"

"Looking for work. Specifically, you." She smiled as Wren stared at her. "Your dad said you might be here. Looks like he was right."

"My dad?" Wren looked mildly horrified now. "Where did you see him?"

"Your house."

"You went to my—!" Wren cut himself off with a sharp intake of breath. "I'm going to kill Rian! You went there because of what he said, didn't you? Why would you do that? Now Dad's going to ask a million questions about you that I'm going to have to dodge, and—why did you even want to find me, anyway?"

"I was hoping you would have some errands for me to do," Dominique said. "I keep getting turned down for employment, which sucks because I came all this way looking for something to keep me and Caspy going. Your dad mentioned that you were going to meet Rian in Risthe-end, but I guess you can't do that now because the trains aren't running, huh?"

"That's not...you really think I told my dad the truth? Seriously?" Wren shook his head. "No, I'm trying to get to Caul-end instead. Rian doesn't actually know I'm coming, but I have something I need to give him."

Dominique recalled what Wren's father had said about their plans for later. Walking to Risthe-end from here was one thing, but Caul-end was on the other side of the city. "You won't be home in time for your dinner reservation if you go now."

"What, did you have an entire bloody conversation with my dad? Did he invite you in for tea too?"

"I think he'd have drawn the line there. He was just angry about you running out on dinner. It's pretty easy to be wealthy, isn't it? He doesn't need to worry about where the next meal is coming from, he just gets to be upset over you missing it."

Wren narrowed his eyes, a perfect match to his father. "If you want to be frustrated with your lot in life, that's fine, but don't take it out on me because my parents happen to have money."

"Oh! Let me guess, because you have your own issues too?"

"I don't have anything of the sort. I know exactly where I'm going. It's laid out for me, my future. University can't come soon enough. Can you say the same?"

He smiled then, a cocky, arrogant thing. No wonder he'd gotten himself punched. Dominique rose to his challenge. "I can't, but at least I'm not lying about that fact."

It had been a bluff, but the smile fell from his face. She'd been listening when Rian said not to trust anything he said, but she hadn't expected it to be *everything* that came out of his mouth. He grabbed

74

hold of his bag's strap, his fingers tapping against it like it was the handle of a guitar. "I can't waste time with you, I have somewhere to be."

"Wait," she said as he went to turn away. "Is it really that important that you get this thing, whatever it is, to Rian?"

Wren eyed her suspiciously. "Why do you care?"

"Because I've got nowhere to be, and like I just told you, I'm desperate for cash. So, how about this? I take whatever it is to Rian, and you pay me to do it. Rian gets his thing, you get to go home in time for dinner, and I don't have to worry about finding another job for today. We all win."

Wren didn't reply immediately. He slung his arm over his bag protectively. After a couple of seconds of thought, he said, "How can I trust you? For all I know, you'll take the money and run."

"Yeah, I could, but I'm not dishonest," Dominique said. The fact that it came from him made it all the more insulting. "What, you've lied so much that now you don't trust other people now?"

Wren let out a surprisingly childish huff at that. He looked back towards the stairs leading up to the platform as if a train might have miraculously arrived there, but it was still as empty as it had been when Dominique arrived. Once he saw that there was no chance of him getting to Caul-end that way, he finally yielded, reaching into his bag. "Fine, you win. Please get this to him as soon as possible. He needs it."

He handed her a small, brown paper bag. Peeking into it seemed like a direct invasion of privacy, but now she was dying to know what was inside. "What is it?"

"Something that could get me arrested by the Politia, Il-or-otherwise," Wren said, looking completely serious. "I mean it. Don't look inside. The less you know, the better."

Dominique examined the bag closely. She knew better than to believe him outright, but now the doubt had been planted in her mind. "Are you sure I should take this if that's the case?"

"Up to you, but how much money do you think delivering something like that is worth?"

She paused, considering. "A lot if I could get in trouble."

"Yeah, I agree. Alright, how about…" He fished around in his bag again, pulling out three distinct notes. "This should be enough."

Dominique's eyes went wide as she laid them on the money. That was the kind of payment for a whole day of serious labour, not a leisurely delivery to Caul-end. She looked back at the brown bag again. "Suddenly, I don't know if this is such a good idea."

"I wouldn't be letting you do it if Rian didn't desperately need it, trust me," Wren said, which was difficult to do when every encounter with him had ended with Rian telling her to do the opposite. He pulled a small book and pen from his bag, tearing a page and scribbling something down on it. "Here. Rian can't be mad at me seeing as he gave my address up first."

She peered at it. "What is this? Is it written in Creilish?"

"What?"

"Seldisian?"

"It's written in plain Harrid!"

"Is it? I can't read it." She turned the page, her eyes beginning to make sense of the looping handwriting. "Oh. Wait, I think I get it, this is where Rian lives? Your handwriting is atrocious."

"My handwriting is fine! You and Caspian both…ugh. Just get that thing delivered. I wasn't lying when I said I needed it there quickly."

Having said his piece, he turned and stalked out of the station, hopefully to go home. Dominique pocketed the money and tested the weight of the bag. There was nothing for it; she'd made her decision.

Now she just had to get it into Rian's hands.

The note from Wren took her to a dingy borough that wasn't far from where she and Caspian lived. It was a deeply impoverished area where children played on the streets, dressed in little more than rags. The homes were less houses and more single adjoining rooms, hardly enough space for two people, let alone a family. Dominique and Caspian had done everything they could to avoid living in a place like this, but they barely scraped by as it was.

Clutching the brown bag to her chest, she avoided the stares of the children and the homeless. Some might have been Ilia themselves, but she didn't dare look close enough to find out. It wasn't that she felt out of place—she and Ezra had both grown up in similar conditions—it was just that she'd been away from it all long enough to forget the reality.

Aquiline was cruel to those who weren't fortunate.

Rian's home was a dull building made of brick that sat on the end of the street. At least, according to Wren's elegantly penned note it was, but his needlessly extravagant handwriting could have said anything. Praying that she'd read it correctly, she went up to the door and knocked.

To her relief, it was Rian who answered. He looked vastly different in his own space, unguarded and dressed in even scruffier clothes than normal. He held a battered sketchbook under his arm as he leant against the door, his eyebrows halfway up his forehead.

"Not the caller I'd have expected," he muttered, shoving a stubby pencil behind his ear. "What in the name of the splits are you doing at my place, lass? Where'd you even get this address?"

Dominique considered asking to come in, but decided it would be too forward of her. Even if it wasn't, she didn't want to linger long. "Here, I'm here to deliver this from Kinglet."

She thrust the bag at Rian as if it was a ticking bomb. Rian took it and peered inside, his features softening. "That sneaky bastard! Why'd he send you?"

"The trains weren't running, and I happened to be in the right place at the right time, so I offered to take it for him." Dominique glanced down at the bag, hoping he'd take the hint. When he didn't, she said, "So, uh. What is it?"

"You didn't take a peek? Weren't even the slightest bit nosy? What did our Wren say was in it?"

"Something dangerous. He said not to look because I'd be safer that way."

Rian snickered. "And you believed him, did you?"

"Of course not! It's just, he offered me a lot of money to carry it, so I figured it had to be something serious."

Rian shook his head in an amused fashion, opening the bag and pulling out a small bottle filled to the brim with green liquid. "It's a medicine, lass. My dad's real sick, see, and I've been on at him to get his parents to help. You know the Sharp family, right? They're proper prestigious doctors, well known in their field, but they won't do jack shit for us. Looks like he stole this from them."

He stopped, staring at the bottle. Dominique was about to ask what was wrong, but didn't get the chance.

"I'm kind of surprised," he admitted.

"Why?"

"I didn't expect him to do anything, honestly."

"I wouldn't have expected it either," Dominique said, taking the bottle and gently swishing it. The colour reminded her of a *triash,* a rare stone that was born from the sentient souls of splits, the magical realms that gave Ilia their power. The tiny artefacts could amplify the magic of its matched Ilia tenfold, but Dominque had never found her own.

"Wren can be a decent enough person when he puts the effort in. It's what I've been trying to encourage." Rian took the bottle back, grinning. "If you see him before I do for whatever reason, let him know I'm over the moon. Thanks to you too, Domi, for coming all this way to get it to me. Means a lot, and I'm serious about that."

His gratitude warmed her in a way she was unused to. Usually, she burned, angry and passionate and furious. This was different. It was the kindness of a stranger, of someone who had no ties to her past, of someone she'd been able to help in her own way.

"You're welcome, Rian," she said, smiling too. "Anytime."

CHAPTER 10

As days passed by with no sign of Ezra, Caspian began to wonder if Dominique's encounter with him had been a dream or a hallucination, just some fickle fear that had come to life. To think that way was to lull himself into a false sense of security, but he needed it as they continued to scrape money together little by little.

Maybe, he hoped, Ezra would never find them. Maybe they had enough time after all.

Their small jar of savings had grown, bolstered by Caspian's not-quite-legal job with the blacksmith. He'd petitioned him for further work, promising to keep it under wraps, to keep his head down and not get caught. It was a risky game for both of them, but difficult for the blacksmith to say no—he apparently had no-one else to call on, and Caspian did good work.

Still, it was disheartening to see just how slow-going it really was. Though he hadn't expected it to happen overnight, just glancing the jar's way made his mood plummet. To start anew, pack up and run, it took more than they were earning.

"It's alright," Dominique said when she caught him staring at it. "Just need a few more odd-jobs like that one for Kinglet, and then we'll be okay. He paid well enough, right?"

She'd come home happier than he'd seen her in a long time after she'd done the job for Wren Sharp, her smile warm and her demeanour bright. She'd hoped to ask after more errands, but both he and Rian had seemingly vanished from Aquiline's streets entirely. When Caspian suggested a trip to The Otherground in search of them, they'd only found Cami and Dane there, Rian's usual stall empty.

"Not seen either of them around," Cami said, looking pensive. "It's odd, 'cause they're always here. Rian might not have any money, but Wren always pays his way for him. Wish I could tell you where they are. Splits, I wish I knew myself."

Nobody else seemed to know where they were either. Though Dominique still had Rian's address, Caspian felt like knocking on his door was too much of an invasion of his privacy when they were just looking to scrounge cash off of him and his friend. In the end, they made the decision to let the matter go. Wren and Rian had their own lives to live, and they'd show up again when it suited them. That was how it was.

A further three days after that trip to The Otherground, Dominique met him after work with a grin on her lips. She crashed into him with a hug, heat radiating off her that warmed his frozen blood after a day of using his power to cool metal. The sun beat down on both of them, but he didn't pay it much mind.

"Hey Domi," he said, hugging her back. "Good day?"

"Best day." Dominique sounded giddy, "Roverest Docks, you know it? I've got myself a job for a couple of nights down there. I won't be back 'til real early morning, but the pay? Super good for what it is. I know it's only a few nights, but it's a boost that we need!"

How did she want him to celebrate it with her? He thought about picking her up, spinning her around in delight, but there was no strength left in him and he wasn't certain if she wanted to be touched like that. Instead, he knocked his forehead against hers, allowing her joy to warm them both through with its pleasant brand of heat. More work meant more money, and more money meant they could get out sooner.

"Good job, Domi," he said. "Maybe we'll do this after all."

"Oh, we will," Dominique said, stepping back. "Before you know it, we'll be out of here."

In that moment, it was like Ezra didn't exist and they were all the better for it. Dominique looked healthier before him, like she could power the sun itself if she wanted, and he too felt like some of the weight had been lifted from his shoulders. She grabbed his hand, still smiling. "Come on!"

"Hm?"

"Let's go!"

"Where?"

"Somewhere fun!"

They didn't go home. Dravendale Park was nearby, and so they went there to watch the deer at Dominique's request. It wasn't much of a spectacle in terms of wildlife, but it was an enjoyable distraction from the smoggy city. Together, they trekked around its entire perimeter, basking in the sun and trying not to spook the animals that roamed around.

When they finally stopped to sit by the lake, Dominique said, "Where do you want to go after we get the money together?"

Caspian peered into the water. He could see himself reflected back in its still surface, his eyes blue and his hair streaky. It was still considerably brown, but that would change in time. Dominique's was almost entirely red, and he knew well what that meant.

But she hadn't asked him how long he thought they'd live. She'd asked him *where* he wanted to go, and he owed her that answer. Now was the time to look to the future instead of dwelling on the inevitable, so he said, "Somewhere quiet, I think."

"The country, then? That suits you, Caspy. Me too, actually…yeah. A little town, not busy, where there's no-one to bother us and we can get fresh bread in the morning. Stable jobs too, something normal. I don't want to have to fake a license."

"Small house," Caspian said absentmindedly. "Away from the markets and the bustle, where we can just be ourselves."

Dominique rocked forwards, grabbing his hands. "There'll be

other Ilia too, so we'll fit right in. Yeah, let's put this hideous city behind us."

He could envision it. Putting it into words gave it power, giving life to the future they so desired. No more threats, no more running from ghosts. Maybe, in their new lives, they would heal, and he would find it in him to tell Dominique how he truly felt.

The sun sank, casting an orange glow across the sky. They'd have to go soon if Dominique wanted to be on time for her work at the docks, but the moment felt too serene, too peaceful. He feared that if they left now, they may never find another like it.

"You okay, Caspy?" Dominique said when he remained quiet.

"I am," he replied. "I know it's time to go, but...just a few seconds longer. Then I'll walk you to the docks, if you want."

"Oh! Such a gentleman, Caspy!" Dominique laughed, but she looked pleased nonetheless. "Alright, a couple of more minutes, I can spare that. Shame that I didn't bring my cards..."

"Such a shame," Caspian laughed, relieved that he wouldn't be thrashed again in several games that he didn't fully understand the rules to. Deer darting across the greenery caught his eye, frolicking with one another, and he smiled. "Yeah, we definitely need to go somewhere in the country...this sort of sight, every day, I think it would do us good."

It was in reach. His magic hummed excitedly at the thought, smiling with him.

The front door was ajar when he arrived home.

Caspian stopped abruptly as he realised, the air around him growing cold. That wasn't right, Dominique always locked the door when she left, she wasn't careless enough to forget. Living in Caulend had taught them to always be vigilant. Those who weren't ended up as victims, as was the way of the district, the way of the city itself.

Hesitantly, he approached, inspecting the door handle first. The entire thing was melted, like someone had taken a hot poker to it. So Dominique hadn't left it open; it was a break-in. His magic reacted to the sight, whispering, whispering. Caspian gave in to it, letting it rise to the surface, ice forming at his fingertips.

If the trespasser was still inside, then he had to be prepared.

He nudged the door open, stepping inside without a sound. The state of the door handle preyed on his mind, all too familiar. Ezra didn't know where they were, he reminded himself, but it seemed too much of a coincidence. An Elementra thief? He could only hope.

Listening for the sound of anything unfamiliar, Caspian held his breath. But there was nothing. Absolutely nothing. Not a single creak or thump, and that only unnerved him more. Like this, his own home felt foreign, too big to contend with. Searching in himself for any thread of courage, he stepped into the main room. "Who's there?"

His blood ran cold. There was someone sat on the windowsill, leant back against the window as if they owned the spot. It took Caspian a moment to recognize him past the horrific scars that twisted his face, but once he did, he felt his throat lock up.

The right side of his chest burned with phantom pain.

"Hey, Caspy," Ezra said gently, sitting up straight. Such a casual movement, but Caspian could see the red in his short hair, the gleam in his eyes that depicted his true nature. "Long time no see."

Anything Caspian might have been about to say died in his mouth, rotting like a corpse. He had to move. Turn back. Get out. But he couldn't, not when his limbs were frozen solid. Ezra Purnell looked worse than he'd ever seen him, a shadow of the overpowering man Caspian remembered. Now, he was thin. Sickly. *Wrong.*

"Cat got your tongue?" Ezra asked as he stood up. "Shit, it's getting cold in here. Hey, don't freak out on me, I'm not going to hurt you, I swear."

Lies. It was all lies. Caspian knew Ezra would turn on him if he made the wrong move, and yet seeing him here now, he didn't seem like the monster Caspian knew him to be. Instead, he sounded a little more like the man he'd once called his friend.

If he fell for the illusion, it was all over. Forcing the words out, he asked, "Why are you here, Ezra?"

"Didn't Domi tell you that she met with me? She ran off, so I had no choice but to come to you." A flash of irritation crossed Ezra's face.

"Weren't that hard after asking around a bit. Had a few run-ins with the Ilpol, but I dealt with it. You know how it goes. I fix things, that's what I do."

Caspian kept his eyes on him, resisting the urge to look away. "You didn't 'deal with it' Ezra."

"What?"

"You killed them. They were just doing their jobs and you killed them!"

"Because they were getting in my way," Ezra said, as if that justified it. "I had to find you. I had to be with you both again."

Caspian shifted, moving aside. "No. You need to go."

"What?" Ezra sounded genuinely surprised. He stepped closer, catching Caspian by the shoulders as he tried to dodge past him, forcibly moving him. Caspian tensed at the contact, trying to resist, but Ezra was still stronger despite how his magic had worn away at him. "Why...? Why do the two of you keep trying to get rid of me? Do you know how hard I looked for you? Do you know how much I've *done?*"

In a heartbeat, their positions had been switched, Ezra with his back to the door, Caspian trapped in the room. Dangerous ground. He took a shallow breath. "You killed people, Ezra. Even you have to know that it's unforgivable. You can't think—"

"Why didn't you come looking for me?" Ezra cut him off. His touch was hot; Caspian would end up burned if he didn't do something. "Why didn't you even try to find me? I searched for months only to find that you'd both moved on. You *forgot* about me like I didn't matter! Why would you do that to me?"

"Because we thought that you were dead!" Something sparked within, something Caspian hadn't felt in a while; raw fury. Coating his hands in his own ice, he grabbed Ezra's hands and threw him off. "We thought you died in that fire, but we didn't forget you. I wish we could. Maybe then we could heal from everything you did to us!"

Silence. Caspian stepped back as Ezra's expression turned cold. He'd said too much, made a terrible mistake.

"What I did to you?" Ezra repeated, slow and dangerous. "What *I* did to *you?* I fucking helped you! I got you to figure out your magic, I showed you what you could do with it. I kept you from screwing things up and I tried to get you on the right path! You think I hurt you on purpose? I was only trying to save you both!"

"Don't lie to me, you—!"

Ezra pulled him close, silencing his protest in a suffocating embrace. Caspian stiffened, realising what he was doing, his anger only stoked by it. It wasn't a show of affection. It was a way of trapping him, of establishing his control.

"Don't fight with me," Ezra said, his voice low. "It's not on me, right? It's this power inside, and it screams, so much sometimes that I can't keep a lid on it. You know that. You have to understand. Domi didn't. I tried getting through to her, but she just didn't get it."

Caspian said nothing. Ezra continued. "You look so different now, Caspy. Your hair and your eyes, they're so pale...I saw it with Domi too. You guys weren't doing well without me, were you?"

Wash it away. Caspian could feel his power, alright. He clenched his fists as Ezra continued to speak in that calm tone, carefully choosing his words. "Don't worry. We're going to figure this all out. You think I'd let the people I love suffer?"

"You would."

"What?"

Reaching up, pushing all the cold that he could into his hands, Caspian shoved Ezra back with all the strength he had. In his surprise, he let go, stumbling back. The room plummeted further in temperature; their breath visible now with every exhale. "I said that you would! You tore us apart, got us addicted to our own power, and that wasn't even the end of it! I don't care what you thought you were doing. Can anything ever justify the way you pushed us around? The way you hurt us?"

For a second, Caspian though he'd gotten through to him. Ezra seemed, stunned. Wordless. Maybe something had changed. Maybe he'd finally realised the kind of damage he'd done to the people he claimed to love.

But then he spoke, his voice icier than even Caspian's magic. "Is your little show over now? Is that it? Out of things to say, or are you not done yet? No. Go on. I'm waiting."

Any hope that Caspian might have had withered and died. Ezra hadn't listened. He never did, unless what he was hearing reinforced his own, twisted views.

When Caspian gave no reply, he laughed, an ugly sound in his throat. "To think I thought that I saw fire in you just then, Caspian. It wasn't me who ruined you. You did that all by yourself. I only taught you how to have fun with your magic, but you were the one who let it overwhelm you. Look at you. How long do you even have left?"

He couldn't think about the answer. If he let Ezra get to him now, it was over. "It's none of your business. It stopped being your business a long time ago."

Ezra reached out to him. "Come on, don't be like that. What happened between us three, it's all water under the bridge now. We can be together again, just like before. Me and Dominique and you. Don't you want that?"

"Burn your bridge," Caspian said. "Get out of our lives."

Ezra started towards him, but Caspian had enough experience to know what came next. He dashed forward, ducking beneath his arm, using his smaller frame to his advantage. All he needed to do was to get past Ezra, and then he could escape.

He wasn't fast enough. Ezra caught him by his hair and yanked him backwards. Pain shot through his scalp, but before he could make a sound, Ezra had him by his shoulders. His back hit the wall as he was thrown against it, but when he tried to move, there was nowhere to escape too. Ezra blocked him from the front, his arms either side of him, caging him there.

His mind flashed back to the day that Ezra had scarred him, the day that everything had burned. It had begun like this, in anger and in fear.

Not for the first time in his life, Caspian was afraid that Ezra might really kill him.

"Why can't I get through to you?" Ezra asked, his voice dangerously calm even as he slammed his fist into the wall by Caspian's head. He flinched in response. "Why can't either of you see that you belong with me?"

Caspian had nothing to say. His heartbeat was out of control, just as his magic was, ice forming all over his skin like a barrier.

"Hey, don't be scared," Ezra said, softening his tone. Caspian knew not to be taken in by it. Ezra was so, *so* talented at making himself sound harmless, but he could feel the heat radiating from his skin and he knew that they'd both burn at the end of it. "We're going to wait for Domi to come home, and we'll be fine. The three of us."

Dominique. He couldn't let her come home to this, to walk into a trap of Ezra's making. Things could never go back to the way they were.

There could never be a *next time.*

His hands found Ezra's throat as he channelled every last ounce of magic into his fingertips, icy enough to hurt. Ezra snarled as he grabbed for him, but Caspian had seen it coming. He let go and shoved Ezra hard enough to send him stumbling back, bringing his hands back in close as he formed a ball of water between his palms.

"You little—!" Ezra covered his neck where Caspian had touched him. "I wasn't going to hurt you! What'd you go and do that for?"

"Don't come near me," Caspian said, holding the ball of water out like a warning. "If you move, I'll…"

"You'll what?" Ezra's eyes flashed, burning, just like his magic. "You're too weak to do anything, Caspian. You always were. Go on. Do something. You know you won't."

Each word struck like a physical blow. Caspian couldn't let himself think. He let himself be fuelled by instinct, the water changing shape in response. It broke apart, freezing into five, spear-like icicles that hung in the air.

"Ezra," he said. "Get out of my house."

A grimace, and then a smirk. Ezra's lips pulled back to reveal his teeth, and as he moved forward, Caspian threw his arm out. No time to aim. No time to consider. The icicles moved at his command, hurtling through the air.

One came close enough to Ezra's face to slice open his cheek, leaving a fine, red gash in its wake. A second embedded itself in his thigh, stopping him in his tracks as he dropped to his knees. The final three embedded themselves in the far wall, Caspian's aim not steady enough to make them all hit.

But it had been enough to down him. Having granted himself an opening, Caspian ran, making his way for the door, hands fumbling to yank it open.

"Caspian!" Ezra shouted after him. "Caspian! Get back here!"

Never. He couldn't stop. Not now.

CHAPTER 11

Carenshiv Market was dead at night. Caul-end's only decent marketplace was usually a bustling mess of people in the day, but as Caspian ran through it, all that was left was its rubbish and countless abandoned crates.

He had no destination in mind, no real place to go. All he had was his adrenaline, which was fading fast, and his magic, which was already starting to attack him for drawing on it once more. He needed a little more time, just enough to slip away, and then it could bombard him all it wanted—but not yet, not when Ezra was no doubt tailing him.

He was so caught up in escaping that he'd stopped noticing anything around him. All the wind went out of him when he slammed into something at full speed, someone *else* who'd stepped out in front of him. The collision sent them bouncing off of one another, crashing to the floor. Caspian winced as his hands scraped against the cobbled street, and for a second, his mind went blank.

Was it Ezra?

But then he looked up and found Wren Sharp inspecting his own hands with a wince. He'd taken Caspian at full speed, and it had left him with grazed palms. His messenger bag had fallen open too, a couple of clear, empty bottles having spilled out onto the pavement.

"Are you *serious*?" Wren hissed. His eyes were empty, cold, no life to them at all. The bruise on his face had faded, but traces of it remained. "Caspian? What are you doing here?"

"Help me," Caspian said, scrambling to his feet. There was no time to explain, or to ask Wren the same question. "He's chasing me, and I can't do this on my own."

The words were a rapid mess. It was a surprise that Wren even understood him. He gathered up his empty bottles, straightening his bag out as he stood. "Who's chasing you?"

"Ezra. He's the one who burned down Mellingdale! He broke into our house, so please, help me."

Wren's eyes flicked to the right, where several crates were stacked. "Is that so? Alright. You hide, and I'll deal with your friend."

"You'll what?"

"I'll deal with it," Wren said, gesturing to the crates. "Now do you want him to find you, or what? Hide!"

Caspian didn't need to be told twice. He darted away, tucking himself behind the pile. He tried to calm his breathing as he made himself scarce. If Ezra heard him now, it would all have been for nothing.

Wren. What was he doing here now? After so many days of being mysteriously absent, he'd finally shown his face—at night, when Caulend's most unsavoury citizens prowled about. He was taking a thousand risks by walking around alone, especially dressed as well as he was. All he needed was the wrong person to spot him, and he'd be mugged for everything he had.

Did he just not care about such an outcome?

Rushing footstep drew his attention. Caspian's heart stopped at the sound. Daring to peek over the crates, Caspian found Wren leant against the wall of the building across the street while Ezra stalked right past.

Wren's gaze followed him as he went. It didn't take long for Ezra to realise he was being watched. "You," he said, turning and marching over to him. "You got a problem?"

"Do you?" Wren asked. "You don't look well. That's a nasty cut you've picked up, had a rough night?"

With Ezra's back to him, Caspian couldn't make out his expression, but it wasn't difficult to imagine his scowl when he spoke. "Damn rich boys, hanging around thinking they own the place...tch. You see a water Elementra go past here?"

Wren gave a lazy shrug. "What if I did? Why'd you want to know?"

"He's hurt, and I'm trying to help him." It was a poor lie, made poorer by the fact that Ezra's face had to be still bleeding. The chunk of ice that Caspian had thrown at him was no longer embedded in his thigh, but it must have still hurt. "Talk. Have you?"

Wren glanced around, like he was thinking his answer through. Ezra clenched his fists. "Stop wasting my time and talk!"

"Yes," Wren said, and Caspian gripped the edge of the nearest crate hard. "I have."

No. He'd trusted Wren. Rian had said time and time again not to, but Caspian had thought that maybe there was something more to him, something worth believing in. After what had happened in The Otherground, after he'd helped Dominique, he'd thought that Wren could be good.

But now he was about to sell him out, and Caspian couldn't stay.

"Where?" Ezra asked. His voice was too close.

"Down that way."

Caspian stilled as Wren pointed well away from the crates, still wearing that empty expression. "He went bolting past me, and he seemed in a right panic. I wouldn't want to encounter whatever it was that spooked him, not with that look in his eyes."

Caspian breathed out, nearly collapsing against the crates. Of course. Wren loved to twist the truth and make up stories, that was why he'd offered his help in the first place. It was for fun; he wanted to mess Ezra about as a joke.

Ezra, however, didn't move. Instead, he stood there, his back to Caspian, shoulders squared for a brawl. He knew. He knew he was being played, there was no way he didn't realise, and Caspian could only hope that Wren knew what he was getting himself into.

"What? Is my information not good enough for you?" Wren asked.

"No. What's up with you?" Ezra closed in, getting up in Wren's face. "What's that smug look for? You don't belong here, rich boy, so what's got you looking like the cat with the cream?"

Wren didn't look at all affected. In the low light of the streetlamps, he seemed different; sharp angles, cutting features, utterly untouchable. "I think you're seeing things. Not that it surprises me, the way you look. Ilia addicts never last long, that's the truth of it."

The words were biting, but he was smiling now, a hint of excitement on his face. Caspian wanted to rush out and shake him. He had no idea what kind of fire he was stoking with comments like that.

"You should learn to watch your mouth," Ezra replied, his voice low. "You don't know who you're talking to."

Caspian would have backed down by now, but Wren didn't seem to fear him at all. "Don't I? You're lucky I even told you where that Ilia of yours went, seeing as it's obvious that you're not *looking* for him. You're chasing him, aren't you? Why?"

"That's none of your business." Ezra said. What was Wren playing at, goading him the way he was? Ezra was a bomb, waiting for any opportunity to explode, and if Wren wasn't careful, he was going to get caught in the blast.

"No, it's not." Wren said, still smiling. "Well, I told you where to go, so how about you move on? I can only hope he gives you a piece of his mind when you find him. Something tells me that you deserve to be taught a lesson of your own."

His words lit the fuse. Ezra grabbed him by his jacket and shoved him against the wall, just as he'd done to Caspian in the house. For a fraction of a second, Wren's mask fractured, his eyes widening.

"You piece of shit," Ezra muttered, and his hands must have been burning. Caspian knew they were. "You better not be lying about any of this, or I swear to every split in this city that the Ilpol will find your charred corpse on the side of the street."

Caspian moved, intent on helping. He couldn't just stand by and let Wren be hurt when he'd stepped in to help him.

But then, Wren's voice, saccharine sweet, made him stop. "No lies here, I swear to you. I only ever tell the truth."

Ezra dropped him. "You better hope that's true too, or else I won't forget this."

Wren leant back against the wall for support, his smile grim as he adjusted his light jacket. "Sure. Have a nice night."

Ezra muttered something beneath his breath before storming off in the direction that Wren had pointed out. Caspian stayed still, waiting until he was absolutely sure he was gone before coming out. His hands shook even though he'd never been in danger. Had he really been that scared for Wren?

Wren looked over at him as he emerged, letting out a breathless laugh. "You really were going to come out to 'help' me there, weren't you? I had it under control."

"Sorry, I just thought…" Caspian shook his head. "No, never mind. Thank you. For saving me, I mean. Because you really did there."

Standing straight, Wren scoffed. "No, thank *you*. I think that was exactly what I needed tonight."

He made to leave, but Caspian reached out, grabbing him by the arm before he could get far. Wren glanced over his shoulder in confusion, but Caspian had made his decision. Now he had no choice but to follow through. "You've been missing for a couple of days. Me and Domi looked, but we couldn't find you. Is everything alright?"

Wren smiled tightly, pulling his arm free. "Yeah, I'm fine."

Caspian knew better than to believe it. It was one of the oldest lies in history, and Wren had to know that. Something wasn't right with him, so Caspian walked around in front and said, "Did something happen, Wren? Is that why you're in Caul-end by yourself?"

At the question, Caspian saw something in Wren's expression that wasn't smug, or arrogant, or irritated. Finally, for the first time, he saw something true; the briefest display of agony before it was gone.

He turned his gaze away. Clearly, it was something he didn't want Caspian to see, and when he spoke, his voice sounded dead, like someone had drained all the energy from him. "It was Tomas…Rian's dad. We couldn't do anything. I thought things might get better if we got him the medicine, but it just got worse afterwards. The days kept going by, but nothing else was helping. I stayed with him until…"

Caspian knew about the medicine because Dominique had told him about it. Wren didn't need to explain everything for Caspian to get the gist of why he or Rian hadn't been around for the last few days. Reaching out, he hoped that maybe he could offer some sort of comfort, but Wren dodged him instead, taking a step back.

"Don't," he said. "I don't need your pity, and I don't want it either. It isn't my place to be upset. It wasn't my dad. Rian's just…Rian's not okay. We reported it and everything, but after they arrived to…after they took the body away, Rian made me leave. I wanted to stay, but he made me fucking leave."

The swear sounded wrong in Wren's upstate accent, jarring and awful. In the same breath, he continued. "Whatever. Just forget it. This isn't about me. Your friend, Ezra, whatever his name was, I've screwed him over. The Ilpolitia are swarming all over where I sent him, still investigating the death of that head inspector. With the state he looks, they'll pick him up. I bet he did it anyway. Just go somewhere safe, Caspian. I need to get going too."

"So soon?"

"Yeah. I haven't been home in days. My parents are going to kill me."

He walked past him again, but Caspian couldn't just let him go, not when he looked so torn up. "Your parents are always angry with you, aren't they? You always say you're going home to a fight."

"It's nothing. Just a normal evening in my house, it's fine."

"But it's not normal," Caspian said, not knowing how he was sustaining his courage, but not wanting to waste it either. "You have to know that it isn't just 'fine'. You're lying again, aren't you? Rian says you do it all the time, but why?"

"Because it's fun," Wren said, sounding irritated again. He hadn't turned around, but he had stopped dead in his tracks. "What point is there in the truth when it's all so boring?"

"That's the shoddiest lie you've told me yet." Caspian didn't understand. How could someone who was so wealthy, so privileged, be so twisted up inside? "You've only got one friend, haven't you? Dane said that your reputation is in tatters. Nobody likes you because nobody trusts you, so why do you keep it up?"

"Because I can't be perfect!" Wren whirled around to face him, anger scrawled across his features. Caspian flinched at the intensity of his words. It sounded honest, perhaps the most honest Wren had been with him so far. "I don't expect you to understand, so forget it. No one gets it."

"Let me try. You let Rian in, don't you?"

He thought Wren might snap at him again, but he didn't. Instead he looked away, tearing a hand through his hair. "My parents, they're doctors, some of the best in their profession. Isaac and Olivia Sharp. Do you know of them?"

Caspian shook his head. He'd never lived in Nadre-end, and any medical attention he'd received certainly hadn't been from those with a licence to practice.

Wren laughed. "Oh, how nice. I wish it were that easy for me. They're...strict. Perfectionists, the both of them. Anything less than the best isn't worth it, but nothing I do is ever any good. I'm *always* doing my best, I'm always trying, but they don't acknowledge it. For them, I'm always with the wrong people, in the wrong places, doing the wrong things—so I just lie to them about it all. It's easier, and it gets them off my back. Thing is, they want me to be like them, but I'm not that intelligent. I don't get sciences, I don't understand the human body the way they do, I can't remember all the names and the processes and I can't do it. I can't do what they can, but I want their approval so badly that I can't just give up."

He stood there, bringing one, grazed hand to his mouth like he wanted to cover over it to stop himself talking. It was difficult for Caspian to comprehend. Nobody had ever had any expectations of him. His own parents had been like him, poverty-stricken Ilia just trying to deal with their own power. That was all that ever mattered for people like them.

"I had no idea..." Caspian said, at a loss for what to say. "It's just...I don't know, why carry on lying? No one else is pressuring you, not the people you lie to outside of your parents."

"But...how can I trust anyone else?" Wren didn't look confident, just broken, a little self-aware for once. "When people know too much about me, I become weak. I lie so much that it's become who I am. The stories, the games, I don't want anyone to know who I am beneath it all, because I'm just..."

He stopped, taking a shuddering breath. "Stupid. I'm so stupid.

Someone offers me their ear, and here I am, spilling my guts up like some insecure kid. Forget this, I'm done."

His actions and words were contradicting one another. He was volunteering information of his own accord even though he'd claimed to hate doing so. Caspian had to know. "Why tell me?"

"Because, despite everything, I think you're trustworthy," Wren said, the words trembling around an uncertain laugh. "You don't seem to expect anything from me. You're just some Ilia addict who showed up out of the blue. When I'm speaking to you, you don't get angry or laugh, you just ask me for the truth."

It wasn't the answer he'd been expecting, but it warmed him to hear it nonetheless. "That's not a lie, is it? You mean that? Even though we haven't known each other long, you trust me?"

Wren grimaced. "Believe it, or don't, it makes no difference to me." He turned his back again. "I really need to go. You do too. Don't go home, that Ezra bastard knows where you live and he might come back. Find somewhere safe and stay there. Or find Dominique. I don't know."

He walked away before Caspian could even say goodbye, leaving him alone in the street, his head a hurricane of thoughts and concerns. Knowing that he was right, Caspian returned home briefly to grab their jar of cash—thankfully untouched—and to jam the door shut. Once he was done, he went down to the docks and sat nearby, intent on waiting for Dominique through the night.

Better she heard it from him than someone else. Better he took her somewhere safe then let her return to the place where Ezra might find them.

CHAPTER 12

The newspapers in the morning were headlined with talk of murder once again. A pair of Ilpol killed the night before, set alight just like the ones before them. Aquiline was dealing with a spree killer, it seemed—one that Dominique Delacroix happened to know intimately.

She'd gotten out of work to find Caspian waiting for her, wearing a haunted look that spoke volumes about what had happened to him. He'd explained it all, that they couldn't go home, that Ezra had been waiting in their living room, and that it was all over. They were backed into the corner once again.

It had been inevitable. She knew that, and yet it still hurt to hear. Ezra would never have just stood by and let them go, but now he'd declared war. More than ever they needed to run, but, where could they go when their savings couldn't get them out of the city?

Caspian's answer to that came in the form of his work. Despite everything that had happened, he still wanted to go, claiming they needed the money more than ever. She saw him off, and then decided that, instead of waiting around, it was finally time to go to the Ilpolitia's Offices in Risthe-end. It wasn't much of a walk from the blacksmith's dwellings, so she set off immediately, sorting through the information in her mind.

They knew for certain that Ezra was in Caul-end, so if she gave the Ilpol enough of what she knew, maybe they'd finally take action and catch him. He'd killed so many of their own that they had no choice *but* to do something. Every time the regular Politia had come knocking on her door before the fire, she'd always sent them away with a false smile fixed to her face—but not this time.

She was done pretending that she was fine.

Finding the building wasn't difficult given its notoriety; it was old and worn but still imposing in stature, a centrepiece of the district. Heading inside, she went up to the first desk, slamming her hands down on its surface. The man sat behind it snapped his head up from a stack of papers, rubbing his greying beard with his cigarette-stained fingers. "What?"

"I need to talk to someone about those dead Ilpol. Right now, preferably."

"You and twenty others, love," the man said, jerking his thumb towards the waiting area beside them. When she looked, she realised that almost all the chairs were occupied. "Get in line."

"Excuse me?"

"I said, get in line. Or what, you so far gone that your hearing's screwed too?"

She narrowed her eyes at him but said nothing. If she started an argument now, she'd only be blamed and thrown out. Cutting her losses, she went and sat down on her own chair, taking stock of the others around her. Every single one was a normal person, no Ilia to be seen. She doubted they had any real information to speak of.

She hadn't been sat there long when someone tapped her on the shoulder. Readying herself to argue her reasons for being there, she twisted—only to find herself face-to-face with another Ilpol. A woman with tan skin and long, dark hair; the same woman who she'd met in Mellingdale not long ago.

"Sorry for how Dirk is," she said apologetically. "Good service really isn't his forte. I know you. We met in Ardr-end, didn't we?"

Dominique nodded. "Erica, right?"

"That's me. You're a fire Elementra, right? Dirk should have shot you to the front of the damn queue, not made you wait. Idiot. Come with me, I'll listen to what you have to say."

At least someone was competent, Dominique thought. Erica led her to a separate room with multiple desks, where she took a seat and offered one to Dominique in turn. "Comfortable?"

"As much as I can be."

"Good!" Erica smiled, leaning back in her chair. "Full disclosure, first. I've got nothing to do with Caul-end at all. My jurisdiction is actually over in Ardr-end, but my partner was likely the first victim of our killer, so I'm willing to put in the extra work. Besides, Aidan would have wanted to get one over on Dirk anyway, so, it works out."

"You're the best person in this force right now, Erica," Dominique said, which only made Erica laugh. "Anyway, I'm Domi, and I know exactly who is committing your murders."

She spent the next half hour detailing the events that had led up to the fire in Mellingdale six months ago, how she'd encountered Ezra the day that Erica had been in Ardr-end, how Caspian had come home and found him in their front room. Erica noted it all down, nodding in sympathy when it was appropriate, asking for clarification when she needed it, and never once interrupting.

"You've been through a lot, haven't you, Domi?" Erica said when she reviewed her paper afterwards. "I know our regular lot went to your home several times back in Mellingdale, but you always sent them away. Was that because he made you?"

Burn it down, whispered her magic, daring her to let her flames free. Swallowing hard against the wave of magic, Dominique shook her head, averting her gaze. "No. I was just…protecting him, I guess. He always said that he never meant it, that it was an accident, or he was just angry, and I believed him. Like an idiot, I believed him."

"That's not true. He manipulated you, that's what people like him do." Erica stood up and rested her hand on Dominique's shoulder. "Don't beat yourself up, okay? You've been a great help. I'll pass this all onto the chief immediately."

"Do you think you'll catch him?" Dominique asked as she went to leave. She needed something from the Ilpol, whether that was reassurance or protection. "I know it was my fault for seeking him out in the first place, but do you really think we'll ever be safe from him?"

Erica hesitated. "This guy, Ezra, he's killed our own. My partner, Aidan, he was a good man. A bit spacey, but kind, and now he's probably dead. Jaime too, she was my friend, and Inspector Allan...they didn't deserve what happened to them. We're going to do everything we can. Though I can't offer any guarantees on when, Domi, know that when we do find him, we'll give it our all to take him down. I promise."

It was something to hold onto, as small as it was. A thread of hope —exactly what she needed to carry on.

The Otherground wasn't as busy in the day as it was at night, but it was for the better. Dominique's head was chaotic enough even without the crowds to add to the din. There were a few patrons dotted about the stalls, but nobody of note, so she ignored all of them and made her way to her usual seat at the counter.

"Hey there, sweetheart." Cami waved at her, as chipper as always. "You're becoming a real regular, huh? You doing alright? You look pretty tired."

"It's just been a long day. Do you know any cheap inns or taverns around here?"

"Cheap what now?"

"Inns. Taverns. Long story short, I can't go home because it's too dangerous." It was a shame. Her book from the library was still there, sat beside her bed. She wanted to reread the story she liked one more time before she needed to take it back, but it looked impossible from where she was sat.

Cami tripped over whatever she'd been about to say next. "What? Sweetheart, what happened? Where's your boy, Caspian?"

Explaining the whole situation was too much effort, so she decided to go for the short version. "The guy who is killing the Ilpol is my old boyfriend. He broke into our house and nearly hurt Caspy, so, yeah, it was a rough night."

"Sounds it," came a bitter voice from beside her. She jumped, finally noticing Rian McCarrick sitting next to her, nursing something vaguely alcoholic. He leant over the counter, swishing the drink that he stared into, his eyes rimmed red.

He looked nothing like himself, his usual grin nowhere to be seen, but she knew why. Caspian had told her about what had happened, how the medicine she'd delivered hadn't helped. Though it'd been a long time since she'd lost her own parents, she understood how it felt.

"How are you doing?" she asked.

"You know? Then I'll leave it to your imagination. Who told you?"

"Caspy did. He saw Wren, and Wren told him about it."

"Did he now?" Rian finally took a sip of his drink, wincing. "Must have been playing on his mind too, then."

"I'm sorry the medicine didn't help."

"I'm sorry too," Rian said. "Thanks, though. I just don't know what I'm meant to do now. It's just...shit. It's all shit. Ilpol-killer boyfriend takes the cake though. You sure know how to pick 'em."

"Yeah," Dominique said, because he was right. "I don't know what I'm meant to do either."

She leant back on her stall, looking up at the ceiling as if the answer might be engraved there. Ezra was out in the city looking for them. They wouldn't be safe until the Ilpol got him, or until Ezra wasted away from abusing his magic. By the time that happened, she'd likely be on her own deathbed. It wasn't a comfort.

Her attention was drawn back by a thump on the counter. She looked back down to find a mug in front of her, filled to the brim with froth. Another sat in front of Rian, which he frowned at.

"Right," Cami said, planting her hands on her hips. "There's one rule to The Otherground, and it's that I don't let sad faces sit on those stalls. These are on the house, 'cause you two look like you need them."

"You just made that rule up," Rian said, taking the mug. "But whatever, don't mind if I do."

He downed it in one. Dominique stared at her own drink. "You're serious? For free?"

"It's the little things," Cami said. "A little bit of kindness can save a life sometimes, you know? So I like to believe, anyway. Not that I think giving away a free beer will do anything big, but there's something to be said for spreading goodness."

"Splits!" Rian said. "That's the most disgustingly sappy thing I've ever heard. If Wren were here, I reckon he'd go and drown himself in a keg."

"And so, beer kills someone instead." Dominique picked up her mug. "Well, guess we should drink to something. To getting drunk?"

Rian raised his other glass, which he hadn't finished yet. "Yeah, let's do that. To getting drunk."

He bashed his glass against her mug, and they drank, the bitterness washing away her unease. One moment at a time. Each second as they came. She could do it. Here, she wasn't alone.

CHAPTER 13

Nothing came for free in Aquiline, especially in Caul-end where scoundrels and Ilia dealt in coin and underhanded sleights. Information, magic, or money; all of it could be traded. All of it could be sold.

Ezra didn't have the kind of power that would be in high demand, and he didn't have much in the way of information either. In exchange for what he required, he would need to give up cash, so it was just as well that he had a surplus on him. Two wallets, so kindly donated to him by the Ilpol he'd run into the night before, a little singed, but ultimately still worth something.

The injuries he'd sustained still ached as he made his way through the darkened streets, but what hurt more was that Caspian had been the one to inflict them. Ezra had known that Caspian had the potential to be strong, but he'd never thought that he'd turn that power on him. Caspian had betrayed him without a second thought back in that house. He'd speared him with ice and then taken off as if *he'd* been the victim.

In time, Caspian would pay for it. But that would have to wait until Ezra figured out where Wren Sharp lived. He'd gotten the arrogant boy's identity with ease; giving a quick description of him to the people of Caul-end had them eager to spill his name. *Kinglet,* they called him in jest, a prissy, wealthy Nadre-ender who spent all his time gallivanting around their streets, flaunting his money and telling his lies. Just the thought of him standing there, playing Ezra for a fool, sparked his magic to life. He'd let himself be strung along, and Wren must have thought himself so clever.

That smug smile had never left his lips, now Ezra thought back to it.

Caspian had to have known him. From what he gathered from the Caul-enders, Wren only cared for himself and the people in his immediate circle, so it made no sense for him to throw Ezra off-track in regards to a stranger. Whatever the case, it hardly mattered. As soon as an address landed in his lap, he'd burn his entire neighbourhood to the ground, a just response for such a crime.

His search for information took him the majority of the day, leading him through parts of Caul-end that he'd never been before. Some were curious as to why he wanted to know. Others were suspicious of his bracelet, a hair's breadth away from calling for the nearest Ilpol. He ignored them, and carried on; for every do-gooder, there were five more desperate denizens falling over themselves to talk in exchange for the cash. Bit-by-bit, he built a story around Wren Sharp; the son of two, well-known doctors, friends with one Rian McCarrick, but McCarrick hadn't been around in days. Much of it was useless, but what wasn't was golden.

Burn it all.

The words rang out in his head like an accursed bell. How he wanted to listen to them, to revel in the glory of it all. He'd find Dominique and Caspian and set Aquiline on fire with them by his side. They'd stand from afar and watch it burn, but before that, Dominique would help him do it. She had to feel the same way he did. He'd press her lips to hers and they would go up in flames, the city nothing more than smoke and ash.

She just had to stop fighting the natural order of the world. Her and Caspian both. Ezra knew the truth, that they were magic before anything else, their power given form. He would show them that when he torched Wren Sharp's home, when he went on to rend Aquiline from the inside out.

They would burn bright before they inevitably burned out, and by the splits, he was going to make sure they burned together. Across the street, he spotted another person he could question, so, putting the thought out of his mind, he plastered a grim smile to his face and approached.

Not long now. Not long at all.

CHAPTER 14

Sleep didn't come easily for Dominique after hunting down an inn that wouldn't demolish all their savings in a single night, but that was hardly a surprise. Ezra played on her mind like a bad dream, and the drinks from The Otherground hadn't done a thing to help either. Instead, she stared at the rickety little clock on the ugly vanity that stood in the corner, watching as it ticked towards the time when Caspian would finish his work for the day. She had her own job to attend to soon, but with her focus as shot as it was, she didn't even know if she'd be able to work.

She left the inn at an appropriate time, and by the time she got to the blacksmith's dwellings, Caspian was already waiting for her. He gave her a tiny wave, but she couldn't drag her gaze away from his face. Shadows beneath his eyes exposed his exhaustion; he hadn't slept the night before, and he'd no doubt been working his magic to the bone throughout the day.

She wanted to ask him if he was okay, but the answer was obvious. Instead, she decided to try and brighten his mood. "I've got us a room in Caul-end."

Tension seemed to drain from his shoulders at that. "It's paid for?"

"Yeah, I went around a ton of places looking for somewhere we could afford. It was still pricey, but what can we do?" She gave him a strained smile, but it had hurt, giving over that money when they'd been trying so hard to save it. "Don't worry, I'll deal with it. Take the train back with what I've got left on me. I've got the address written down, okay? Don't walk."

It wasn't that she was concerned about him running into Ezra. It was more that she worried he wouldn't make it back at all. He looked worse than she'd seen him in a while, his eyes all too blue, swimming in magic. Fishing the money out, she passed it to him, alongside a scrap of paper that had the address. He took it, pocketing it before looking back at her.

"What?" she asked.

"You're beautiful."

Heat bloomed in her cheeks. "Where did that come from?"

He looked just as surprised as she felt. "I just...felt like I should say it. Like you might want to hear it."

She laughed, shaking her head in disbelief. "You're too sweet, Caspy. If it means anything, I think you're beautiful too."

Some life crept back onto his face as he gave her a look of mock-offence. "Not handsome?"

"Definitely beautiful," she insisted. It was true; Caspian wasn't handsome in the conventional sense of the word. He wasn't rugged, or muscular, or tall. He was a glass sculpture of a boy, all fine lines and delicate features. Not imposing, not dangerous, simply Caspian Fay, Ezra's opposite.

A thought came to her then, impulsive and hot. Her fingertips burned, and Caspian seemed like water before her. If she touched him, he might fall through her fingers. It couldn't happen, not if she wanted him to burn it all with her. He had to solidify. He had to be *more*.

Burn it down.

"Domi?" Caspian said, eyes wide with concern.

His voice broke her magic's hold. When she looked down at her hands, they were shaking. It hadn't been her. Whatever had thought those things, it couldn't have been her. She didn't sound like that. She didn't think like that.

But it *had* been her. She and her magic were one and the same, and her power was growing impatient. *Burn it down,* it whispered again, and she knew why it demanded.

It wanted to destroy, just like Ezra's did.

Work was laborious, but all the better for it. With her mind occupied, it couldn't stray to darker places, couldn't listen to the hum of her power. She forced herself to focus, dragging containers around the docks even as her limbs protested, tired muscles begging for reprieve. It wasn't right, not when she'd always been a strong girl. Fatigue was starting to become a dreaded familiarity.

When she finished her shift, Caspian wasn't waiting for her. A good sign. Nothing had disturbed him, then. The sun had risen early, and it already felt like it was going to be a scorcher of a day, the rays spilling out over the smoggy city and drying out the air.

She went back to the inn, letting herself in quietly. It was a small room, only one bed, but Caspian had been conservative with the space. He slept quietly, keeping rigidly to one side, the air chilled despite the warmth outside. It was a giveaway; though he looked peaceful, whatever he was dreaming of was giving him a reason to draw upon his power.

Not making a sound, she sat on the bed beside him, daring to reach out and brush his wispy hair from his face. She'd meant it when she'd said he was beautiful, the ice-white that streaked through the strands otherworldly and bright. Ilia magic was such a pretty lie; it took the strong and made them weak. It wouldn't be long before it stole the colour from his hair entirely, before his eyes were overtaken by it. Eventually, he'd look more ill than striking.

Eventually, he'd look like she did.

"When I'm gone," she whispered, the words more breath than sound, "don't you dare follow me. I don't want to see you so soon, Caspian."

Despite her quiet, he still stirred. Putting on a smile, she pulled back from him. "Morning. Good dreams?"

"Yeah," he lied, rubbing his eyes. "Did your work go okay?"

"Sure. Now I'm the one ready for bed."

"I'm *always* ready to sleep."

"Who isn't?" She laid back on her pillow, drawing on her magic. Flames sprung from her fingertips, and carefully, she moulded them into the shape of a bird. The book she had to leave behind sat at the forefront of her mind; maybe she'd have to chance a trip home to find it.

"What's that?" Caspian asked. Dominique turned her head to look at him, watching as the bird's form reflected back in his bright, blue eyes. Sleek body. Thin beak. Fiery wings. "It doesn't look like any bird I've ever seen."

"That's because it's not a real bird, dummy." She made it flap its wings, the heat fanning outwards. "Come on, you know what a phoenix is. Everyone does."

"Oh, like the legends. Right...a bird that's reborn from the ashes. Or is it always on fire? I don't remember."

"Both, sort of. Remember that book I had? It was about old Ilia tales, but there was only one really good one in there." Dominique gazed at the bird, funnelling more power into it to give it life. It raised its head. "It was about a man who wanted only to save his country."

"Thought you only liked books with girls as heroes."

She smiled. "I like any kind of hero. Anyway, the man had a Constra *triash,* this stone that could empower holy magic in the right hands, and the king of his country was a tyrant who could wield Constra too. When he caught wind of this *triash,* he sent his men to retrieve it, so the man took the stone and ran, desperate to keep it out of his grasp."

"A lot of work for one tiny stone."

"A tiny stone with crazy power! So...where was I? Right. He tried to escape them, but eventually he ran out of ground to cover and found himself cornered. In the struggle, the king's men nearly beat the man to death, but..." Her phoenix began to take on a mind of its own, freeing itself of her hands. "As he laid there, beaten and bloodied, something appeared before him. A bird the size of a human being, completely made of flame, its wings wide and burning. It fought in his place, stealing the lives of those who would have killed him, and then vanished again. The phoenix, the immortal bird."

The phoenix stretched its wings. *Burn it down,* it whispered, its beak moving as it threatened to take flight.

Caspian wasn't watching the bird. She realised he was watching *her.* "I've never heard the story before, but it sounds heroic."

"It does, right? But...I don't believe it was just a bird."

"No?"

"What kind of bird would understand the power of a *triash?* What bird would understand that man's plight? The phoenix shows up in other stories too, so my theory is that it was an Ilia using their powers to appear like a bird. A fire-based Elementra like me with their own *triash,* magnifying their powers and helping those in need."

Burn it down. As the phoenix broke free of her, she closed her hand around it, suffocating it before it could start anything. In her chest, she felt the rumbling of an aftershock, a sharp pain lancing through her ribcage. With her free hand, she gripped the blankets.

"We could do with more hero Ilia," Caspian said. "Maybe then, Aquiline would think that we're better."

"You're already hero enough, putting out raging fires." Dominique closed her eyes, exhaustion sweeping over her. "Now, I need to sleep...stay with me?"

"I'm not going anywhere. I'm still tired too."

"Good." She tried to make her mind slow down, tried to make her body relax, but she had no such luck. Instead, she found herself wishing she had a different power. If only she could be more, if only she had the power to make time stand still, or to rewind it, just some way to make their momentary peace last forever.

All she wanted was to bring them a happy ending of her own accord. To be the hero, even just once—it would be the most wonderful feeling of them all.

CHAPTER 15

IN HER DREAMS, THE PHOENIX TOOK FLIGHT, SOARING THROUGH THE SKY like a shooting star, an impossible blur of heat and energy. First, Dominique watched. Then, she looked down at her hands and coated herself in that same energy. She could burn as brightly. She could be as powerful.

She awoke with a start, sticky and overly-hot, the air so thick that it was nearly suffocating. Caspian was gone, a cursory glance at the clock revealing that it had been an hour since he'd left for work. Without him, the temperature had gone back to normal, but for once, that was not a good thing. As the room grew stuffier, her power impacting it, she knew she had to get outside. If she remained, she would burn, she knew as much.

Leaving the inn was like walking into a brick wall, however, the heat just as overbearing even by Dominique's standards. Her hair stuck to the back of her neck, her shirt to her skin. Warm. Too warm.

This wasn't how summer was meant to be.

She leant against the wall, tipping her head back as she tried to calm herself down, to get her temperature regulated again. This was the power she so adored at its worst, rampaging even in her sleep, refusing to be tamed. How she wished she could have fallen in love with something a little less destructive. It simply wasn't in her nature to play it safe; her experiences had taught her that Elementras scorched in fire could not go peacefully. Everything they did was done in extremes, and, just as Ezra couldn't love in moderation, neither could she.

Caspian wasn't safe in either of their hands. She knew that now more than ever.

"'Scuse me, Miss?"

The sleazy voice dragged her from her hazy thoughts. Dominique turned her head to the source, coming face-to-face with a greasy looking man, half his teeth missing when he grinned. Though there were other people on the street, he looked directly at her.

Her skin crawled beneath his gaze. "What?"

"Don't suppose you're Domi Delacroix, are ya?"

"Who's asking?"

"Me. You match what he said. We've been looking for you, we 'ave."

She looked around, trying to find the 'we' he'd spoken of, but he seemed to be alone. "Who's *he*?"

"You already know, don't ya? Got a message for you, love. Said he wanted you to read it with your own two eyes. You or Caspy Fay, he didn't care which one."

He handed her a piece of paper. Dominique snatched it from his grip, unfolding it in a single, swift movement. The handwriting scrawled across it was shaky, near unreadable. It took her several attempts to read it.

Dread pooled in her stomach, heavy and hot. *Whichever of you this gets to first, 24 Cage Street, Nadre-end. You'll find the way. Both of you, meet me there, or I'll burn this entire district to the ground.*

Frozen to the spot, she stared at the words until they became an incomprehensible blur. Her magic buzzed in its rage; the words unintelligible now. When she could take it no longer, she crumpled the paper, her hand a fist around it.

She knew that address. She'd been there before, talking to Isaac Sharp on its doorstep. What business did Ezra have there? Why had he singled out *that* address?

"Look right spooked you do. What's it say?" asked the man.

112

"You didn't read it?"

The man flashed her his nasty, toothless grin. "Nah, I'm only doing what I'm paid to do. Ain't gonna tell me? Well, that's fine by me. I did my job, so I'm out."

He turned his back. Dominique watched him leave, the sun searing her skin, hotter than before. The note said to bring Caspian, but he was still working, and she didn't know how much time she had left before Ezra made good on his threat. He'd already burned Mellingdale; there was no way he was going to pull his punches now.

It was a trap, anyway. She didn't need to read too closely into the note to know that. Bringing Caspian along wasn't an option to begin with.

With no time to waste, she knew she had to move. First, she ran back to the inn, leaving a note of her own for Caspian to let him know she might be back late. With that taken care of, she set off for the station, rushing through the streets, pushing past the people who were about. The heat had drawn everyone outside, it seemed, but now they were just in her way.

As she walked past The Otherground, she came to an abrupt stop. She turned, looking at its inviting doors, and found herself gravitating towards it instead. The thought of telling someone where she was going hadn't occurred to her at first, but she was going to meet with *Ezra*. If she was going to walk into his trap, then the least she could do was tell someone she trusted.

Quietly, she ducked inside. It felt like normal. Cami and Dane made their drinks and tended to their customers, all while Rian sat with his head on the counter, looking like the world had just ended. For Aquiline, it was just another day. Nobody knew what kind of threat Ezra posed now. Nobody knew what was going on behind the scenes.

She walked to the counter, ignoring everyone else around her. "Cami?"

Cami paused in the midst of mixing a drink, looking up at Dominique in surprise. Like she could sense something was wrong, she passed the drink to Dane and said, "What's going on?"

Rian lifted his head, curiosity winning out over his grief, and pulled a face. "Yeesh, lass, you're wearing a face like a widowed wife. Who died?"

She still had Ezra's note in her hand. If Rian found out that Ezra was targeting his best friend's home, she had no doubt that he'd be on the next train out of Caul-end alongside her. She couldn't let him know. Even if she was betraying him by concealing the truth, she couldn't put him in danger too.

"I came to…" Dominique trailed off. What had she really come to say?

"Domi?" Rian looked concerned for once. "You seriously look like you're gonna fall apart."

His casual use of her name jarred her, because it seemed like he'd also realised something was wrong. "I'm going to Nadre-end," she said, the words thick in her throat. "There's something I need to do there, and it could be nothing, maybe it is, but it also might be dangerous. Don't worry about me, I'll be fine, but I just needed to tell someone in case…"

"In case of what?" Cami tilted her head, her eyes inquisitive. "What trouble are you in this time?"

"Screw that," Rian cut in. "What's in Nadre-end? What's happening there for you?"

"Something important," she said, dodging the question as much as she could. "Look, don't worry, just, please, if I don't come back by tonight, tell someone. Alert the Ilpol, or Caspian, I don't know, just… just do this for me. Please."

She turned her back to leave, but as she got to the door, a hand on her shoulder stopped her. When she turned back, she found Cami behind her, her free hand covering that bronze stone she wore around her neck.

"Dominique." Her tone was sombre. "You're worrying me."

It was unfair to keep her secrets to herself. Dominique knew that she shouldn't be weighing Cami down with her own problems, but she needed the help in case things *did* go wrong "Nothing will happen. You won't need to call the Ilpol, I'm sure. It's just a precaution."

Still, Cami didn't look convinced. "Honey, I don't know what's going on with you, and I sure don't know what baggage you're hanging on to, but I need to ask you something. Are you prepared for every outcome? Are you ready to face what's in front of you?"

"I don't know," Dominique admitted, taking a deep, steadying breath. "I don't know what's in store for me, but it doesn't matter. This is something I have to do, and I'll do it, damn the consequences."

Cami smiled, but it was hardly a happy look. "I see. So that's the kind of person you are."

"Cami?"

"Wherever you're going, don't forget your own strength." Cami squeezed her shoulder in a comforting gesture. "Goodbye, sweetheart."

They looked at one another, Cami's bronze eyes staring into hers, the same shade as the stone she wore. What did it mean, if anything?

"I won't forget," Dominique replied, turning her back once more. "Goodbye, Cami."

~

Dominique arrived at Cage Street within the hour, but nothing seemed amiss at first. Several people were in their front gardens, using the heat as an excuse to tend to their plants, and many couples walked arm-in-arm past her. Every now and then, she thought she caught the scent of smoke, but there wasn't any sign of fire. It was simply paranoia. The street hadn't burned yet, and it wouldn't.

She had the power to stop Ezra, and when she found him, she would. There was no use in panicking. Forcing herself to remain steadfast and calm, she pushed onwards to the place where Ezra would be, 24 Cage Street.

Wren's home didn't look any different from afar, and as she approached, she wondered if it had all been a bluff. But no. It wasn't Ezra's style. He wouldn't have gone to all that effort to not go through with it. He'd gone as far as paying off Caul-end's rabble to ger her that message, and that meant it wasn't just a game. He'd never have started something he wasn't intending on finishing.

She was proven right when she walked up the path towards Wren's house. The front door was slightly ajar, as if someone had stepped out with the intention to come back in. Was that why nobody had noticed or bothered to check in? It didn't seem all that strange, and Nadre-end wasn't the kind of place where an unlocked front door would end in a burglary.

She reached forward to push the door open further, only to hesitate at the final second. Whatever was waiting inside, she knew it was nothing good. The Sharp family didn't seem like careless types. She doubted they'd have just left the door open of their own volition.

No use in overthinking. Steeling herself, she went inside.

Crossing the threshold wasn't as momentous as she'd been expecting. Inside, it was a house like any other, just bigger and grander, with more rooms than she was used to. She was out of her depth, yes, but that didn't change the fact that it was just brick and décor, nothing to actually be afraid of. She paused in the hall, listening for the sound of anyone else, but there was nothing. No shuffling. No murmured conversation, no sign of life.

Perhaps Wren and his family weren't home. Maybe they really had stepped out. When she poked her head into the dining room, there was nobody sat around the table. The kitchen was empty too.

The walls held a few paintings here and there, and the carpet underfoot was plush and cream. It was clearly the home of a wealthy family, but it also felt so clinical, the sort of place that Dominique could never live. She spotted a perfect, spiralling staircase that led to a second floor, but before that, there seemed to be a sitting room. Figuring that it would be best to scope out the first floor entirely before heading up, she made for it, expecting to find nothing—and instead froze in the doorway.

Wren Sharp was slumped against the far wall, his eyes closed, completely still. His notebook laid open near him, a single pen astray. Ezra, on the other hand, made himself at home on the nearby sofa, lounging back on it.

She could see the beads of sweat on his forehead, how he was rubbing his hand against his trousers in agitation. Still, his eyes lit up as they fell on her, blazing red.

"Ezra," she said, breathless. "What have you done?"

He smiled, wide, casual and *dangerous.* "Nothing, yet. It's about time you got here, I was just getting bored."

CHAPTER 16

CASPIAN ALL BUT WILTED IN THE SUN WHEN HE FINALLY ESCAPED FROM work.

It sapped at his already limited energy, and, worse still, the long hours of chilling metal had left him too drained to cool himself down internally. Such was the give and take nature of his power. Sometimes, it bolstered him to heights he never knew he could reach. Other times, it left him with nothing.

With Dominique not there waiting for him, he walked home alone. It took double the usual amount of time given the heat and his own exhaustion. The coming of summer meant that he was doomed to spend the next few months sweltering, the dry air taking all the fun out of his magic. She'd like it at least, the only upside.

She wasn't there when he arrived back at the inn. In her place was a note on the bed, penned in hasty scrawl. *'Had to go. Don't wait up. –D'*

Usually, she doodled a caricature of a smile face, or some stick figure of herself running whatever errand she had planned. This time, however, it was blank. Perhaps she'd gone drinking at The Other-ground? If she had, he could always join her. Though he wasn't feeling up to getting drunk himself, he could always just pop his head in, check that she was okay, and then head back. For all he knew, Wren would be there too. He hadn't seen him since the night with Ezra, and he wanted to catch up.

It was beginning to get busy when he arrived, the seats filling up quickly. Dominique wasn't sat up by the counter like she usually was, though, and only Rian seemed to be around. Caspian waved when he looked over his shoulder to see who had approached, but as soon as their eyes met, Rian pushed his half-empty drink aside and moved to get up.

"Hey, Rian?" Caspian intercepted him, stepping in front to block his path. "Have you seen Domi around?"

Rian shrugged. "She was here earlier, looking a right state. Sorry to disappoint, but she's long gone."

Caspian recalled the note, written quickly, no hint of Dominique's humour in sight. "What do you mean?"

"She muttered something about heading off to some kind of danger in Nadre-end, all cryptic-like. Said not to worry though, so I wouldn't bother. No point in wasting energy, right?" Rian smiled grimly, but he didn't look as if he had any energy *left* to waste. His face was blotchy, his eyes red-rimmed. "Whatever. Hope you find her. I've gotta go. Can't keep wasting my money on alcohol when I don't even know how I'm gonna pay rent."

Caspian grabbed him by his shoulders as he tried to walk past him. "No, wait. What do you mean 'danger'? What was she talking about?"

"I don't know. She weren't saying anything, proper cagey-like." He paused, gently removing himself from Caspian's grip. "Hey, don't worry. Domi's a strong lass, ain't she? She'll be fine."

Rian's words meant nothing, not when Caspian knew that there was a very real danger still prowling around Aquiline. The sparse note indicated that Dominique had been in a rush, occupied with something else, and there was only one man who could have spooked her so badly. If it *was* Ezra, then Caspian had no choice but to follow her, even if the thought of seeing him again left him cold.

"I'm going," he said. "If she's in trouble, then I have to find her."

"You're taking action? I didn't think you had it in you." Caspian couldn't tell if Rian intended for that to sound mean-spirited or not. "You got space for one more? Might head over with you and see

Wren, but I can't afford it on my own. They do deals if you have a travelling partner, and trust me, if there's anything I need right now, it's a discount."

If anything, it was a relief. Caspian didn't know if he could face whatever was in Nadre-end by himself, but having a companion strengthened his resolve. "I'm leaving now, is that okay?"

"It's perfect," Rian said. "I've got things that need patching up, after all."

Rian chattered away at him the entire way to the station, and then continued to carry on the conversation even after they'd boarded. It didn't seem to matter that Caspian was barely responding, or that the train itself was hardly comfortable. On the contrary, his nattering just kept getting faster, the nonsense out of his mouth more frequent. It was like he was trying to distract himself from something.

"I usually use Wren for the deals," he said now, animatedly moving his hands to punctuate his sentences. "'Use' is such an ugly word for it though. We've been friends a long time, we have, so he's used to it."

Caspian nodded, only half listening. Rian carried on when he didn't reply. "I didn't mean to get mad at him the other day, you know? It was just…intense. I didn't know what to do and he was saying all the wrong things. He can be insensitive like that, but a lot of the time he don't realise it. It's not like he means it. It's just how he is."

"You hurt him by sending him away," Caspian said absentmindedly. He hadn't quite realised it was as significant as it was until he noticed that Rian had gone quiet. The train carriage they shared suddenly felt more cramped than it was. "Um, I didn't mean…"

"No, is that true?" Rian sounded softer than usual. "How would you know something like that?"

"He told me," Caspian said. Well, he hadn't, but as good as Wren was at lying with his words, his body language had been a different story. "He was upset when I saw him that night."

"Wren? Upset?" Rian laughed in disbelief. "You're bullshitting. He'd never tell anyone if he was hurting."

"I don't think you always need words to be truthful. I don't lie either, so you can believe me on that."

Rian didn't say anything. There was no way that Wren would ever tell him any of that, so Caspian figured it was better that he heard it now, from him. It was a wonder they'd remained friends for so long if they never told each other anything. How did they ever get anything through to each other?

"Rian? I didn't mean to step out of line," Caspian said.

Rian shook his head. "I didn't know he felt that way. He hides everything from me, from everyone. He can't bloody stand it if someone gets in."

"Why do you stay friends?" Caspian blamed his curiosity on his nervousness, on his desire to distract himself from whatever was waiting in Nadre-end. "What do you see in him if he's so dishonest and closed off?"

Rian averted his gaze. "That's none of your business."

Caspian recalled the way Rian had looked at Wren in the bar, the night after they'd first met. Wren had been so dismissive of the idea of a relationship when Caspian had asked him outside, but that look on Rian's face...

"Is it just friendship?" he asked, putting the sparse pieces together in the only way he could.

Rian's expression turned poisonous as he sank into his seat. "Never took you for a nosy good-for-nothing. Mind your own business and I'll mind mine, thanks."

That stung. Caspian knew he'd made the wrong decision by asking. The tension in the air was even more stifling than the heat. Now that Rian had stopped talking entirely, Caspian wished he'd at least go back to chattering his nonsense.

The train began to slow. As they approached Nadre-end, Caspian felt his anxiety settle in his stomach like a stone. Finding Dominique in a district as big as Nadre-end would be like finding a person inside a split. Rian was his only guide, and now they didn't even seem to be on speaking terms.

"I'm sorry," Caspian said. "I didn't mean to pry, really, I just thought..."

"Whatever you thought, it don't matter." Rian sighed, looking out the window. "It's been a tough couple of days. I lost it all, Caspian, and I got mad at him because he just didn't know what to do. He's useless at understanding other people, probably because he never bothers to try. It's a miracle he ever let me in at all."

"I was wondering how you two actually became friends."

"We were kids. I guess I interested him because I was this poor, clueless boy hanging around his pretty district. Maybe he didn't think I was a threat, I don't know." Rian smiled despite himself. "I dunno what I'd do without him, though. As stupid as he is, as cold as he can be, he's still my best friend, Caspian. Sometimes, when it's just us, I get to see the way his eyes really light up, or he'll say something so ridiculous that we both end up laughing our asses off. Then occasionally he'll surprise me by being a half-decent person for once, and I just need to tell him I'm sorry for the other day. I need things to be right again, like it was."

It was, in a way, the answer to Caspian's previous question. The way he spoke about Wren reminded him of the way he thought about Dominique.

Rian frowned, his gaze still drawn to the window.

"Have something more to say?" asked Caspian.

"No, not that. There's something—"

"Smoke?" A young woman sat up straight beside him, her eyes wide. Louder, she cried, "Smoke! There's smoke! Everybody, look!"

Caspian looked. True to her word, black smoke was beginning to rise above the buildings from somewhere in Nadre-end. Not too far from the station, by Caspian's judgement.

"Is that another fire?" someone else said, and his throat went dry at the thought.

And then Rian finally looked back to him, horror written in his features. "I think...I think it's coming from Cage Street. I've been there a hundred times, I know exactly where it is and that's—it's where Wren lives."

Like that, the dots connected. Dominique in Nadre-end, Wren only a few nights ago. He'd sent Ezra in the direction of the Ilpol officers who had then been burned to death.

Ezra's threat still rang in his ears. *"You better not be lying about any of this, or I swear to every split in this city that the Ilpol will find your charred corpse on the side of the street."*

Caspian stood, making for the train's doors, pushing past the people who had gathered by the window. It hadn't stopped yet, but he needed to be off of it as soon as it did.

"There's no time to waste!" he called to Rian as he stumbled his way through the train behind him. "Show me the way. We have to get there *now.*"

CHAPTER 17

THERE WAS ALWAYS ONE RULE THAT REMAINED CONSISTENT IN A WORLD of magic and oddity, and that was that if there was smoke, there was almost always fire.

Dominique could smell it as Ezra sat back in his seat, his arms crossed against his chest. He looked worse than ever; a thin rail of a man who had once been built like a bull, his scars angry, at odds with his calm expression.

"You came alone?" he asked.

"I did."

A bark of a laugh. He sat up. "I planned for that. Both of you are too selfless. Whoever got that note first would be the only one here, 'cause you wouldn't dare tell him, and he'd never tell you. Just means I don't have to feel bad about not keeping my promise, then."

"Promise?" Everything about this was wrong, the heat overbearing and the smell of smoke getting stronger. "What have you done?"

"Nothing that wasn't deserved," Ezra said, his gaze flicking to Wren before snapping back to her. "He picked the wrong fight, but don't start worrying. He ain't dead—yet."

Every word set her nerve endings alight. Ezra leant forwards, clasping his hands in front of him, still too calm, too casual. "You smell it, don't you? You're more sensitive to this kind of thing than the normal lot. See, I set a few sparks down in this street, nothing out of control, but just these tiny, controlled things that are out of sight. They won't blaze until I tell them to, but without Caspy here, I guess there ain't a point in mincing words. This entire street is going down, Dominique, and you're going to watch it with me."

Multiple points where the fire seems to have originated from. That was what the papers had said about Mellingdale too, but she couldn't let it happen here. Even if it meant giving herself over, she had to stop him. There were lives at stake, lives that depended on her talking him down.

Reaching out, she offered one hand to help him up. "You don't have to do this. Just put out the flames and we can figure something out, together. Please, Ezra."

He shoved her hand aside and stood, pressing his hand to his forehead to wipe away the sweat. "I wanted to burn everything with you, you know?"

Flames flickered at the fingertips of his other hand. Small things now, but one wrong move would be all it took for this to turn into a tragedy. "This is mad, Ezra! You can't want to see everything gone!"

"Don't you hear it too, Domi?" Ezra's eyes were so, so red. Who was she speaking to really? Him, or his magic? "I want to burn it all. I want to stand over Aquiline and watch as the flame catches on it, you and me and him. We could own this place. We could watch as it falls."

Burn it down. Her magic answered in her stead, a sign that she was heading down a road she wouldn't be able to turn back on. Still, it was hardly an excuse. If she could fight it, then why couldn't he?

"We wouldn't own anything," she spat. "Is that why you burned Mellingdale to the ground? Is that why you killed all those Ilpol? Is this everything you want, Ezra? To see it all in flames?"

"*With* you," Ezra insisted, that manic look in his eyes. "Today, we start with this street, and when Caspian is here, we'll burn the rest, the entire city!"

It wouldn't have mattered if she'd brought Caspian with. Ezra was going to torch the street, and nothing she did would change his mind —yet still, she had to try one last time. "This isn't you."

"It's always been me," Ezra said, raising his hand. "The same way it's always going to be you."

The flames at his fingers fanned out. Outside, she heard someone scream, someone shout. Voices piled on top of one another and she knew exactly what it meant. Every single one of his sparks had caught. The street was going to go up if she didn't stop it.

She threw herself at him, heat in her hands as she reached for his neck. The momentum sent them both crashing to the floor, the two of them landing hard as Ezra's flames darted away from him, catching on the walls, the nearby table. They all went up immediately, flames rushing up them like they were doused in gasoline. "No!"

"It's all on fire now, Domi!" Ezra snatched her wrists with his burning hands. "At least enjoy it!"

She fought his grip, drawing upon her own power. He didn't let go despite how she burned. "Ezra, stop! If you do this, you'll kill us all!"

"We're not dying here!" Ezra tightened his grip on her, his face still split by that hideous grin. "I survived once, you think I can't do it again? We're going to leave here, you and me! We'll watch this place burn and you'll understand why I did it!"

He pulled her close, pressing his lips to hers. The kiss was rough and blazing, a bid for power rather than a show of love. How had she ever missed this? Wrenching her head back, she slammed her forehead into his, the impact dizzying as it smashed through her temple.

But she'd been expecting it. Ezra hadn't. In his surprise, he let go, allowing her to yank her wrists free of him. She didn't waste any time getting up, but he was quick. As she made it to her feet, he caught her, slamming his arm into his midsection, the blow throwing her back against the burning coffee table.

Her head snapped back from the force. Above her, she saw the flames climbing, burning away at the ceiling. The room was fast filling with smoke, and the entire house would come down in time. They wouldn't survive it. Not something like that.

Ezra stood over her as she tried to recover, his shoulders heaving with rage. "You know what's bad design, Domi?" he asked, his anger barely contained. "Building houses so close together that, if one goes up, all the others will follow. Aquiline can't blame us. They can only blame each other."

She grabbed her own head, trying to regain her bearings. The heat pressed down on her, too much pressure. The smoke was thick and arid as she breathed it in. Wren was still in here. If he didn't burn to death, he'd suffocate.

Pushing herself to her feet, Dominique looked at Ezra, her jaw set in defiance. "This is the last chance I'll give you," she said, echoing words he'd said to her a thousand times before, always the precursor to the Politia knocking at their door in Mellingdale. "Put out these flames, or else."

"If you want this to stop, you have to make me," Ezra replied, matching her gaze with his own. "I don't think you have it in you!"

Focusing her heat in her hands, she rushed him again, aiming for his throat. He twisted away from her grasp, grabbing by her own instead. He wasn't shy about applying pressure, all the breath leaving her as she struggled to draw in more. He was stronger than her. He always had been.

"You think that's *enough*?" he asked. "You want me to stop so bad? Then actually try! You never could then, so what makes you think you can now?"

She was no trained fighter. Ezra was too quick and furious for her to catch through mindless attempts. There was no way to overpower him without drawing upon all of her magic; she couldn't save anyone by continuing to hold back.

He threw her to the floor as she thought she might pass out, and through the smoke, she saw disgust cross his features. "I don't get it, Domi...I try so hard, I try and do everything right, and you reject it every single time! I just want you to come with me, you and Caspian both!"

The oxygen thinned out. She choked as she tried to draw in as much as she could. Ezra continued to look down on her. He *always* looked down on her. If she tore out his eyes, maybe then he'd stop.

"Domi." He knelt down beside her, a gentle look on his face now. "Why couldn't you have done what I said? It would have been so much easier."

Dominique felt something catch alight in her own chest at the words, something raw, something angry, something *hot*. She raised her head and smiled back at him. "That answer is easy."

"What?"

"It's because you were always wrong!"

She threw her hand out in front of her. Her own flames shot forth, unfocused and careless. He wouldn't have expected her to fight fire with fire when she was trying to douse his flames to begin with, and as she hoped, they hit their mark. They caught him across his face, near his eyes. He covered them immediately, an agonised cry escaping his throat.

Now was her chance. She grabbed him by his jacket and pulled him upwards, using all of her limited strength to swing him backwards. He staggered in shock, his body vanishing into the wall of flames that he'd set up himself. His screams were the only sign that anyone was even caught in the blaze.

A nauseating feeling rose up inside her. For a moment she stood there, breathing hard, stunned that she'd done such a thing. Trying not to listen, trying not to imagine the pain he must have been in, she turned and ran to Wren. He didn't seem to be badly injured, and was even beginning to stir to her relief. Judging by the little amount of blood in his hair, she imagined that Ezra must have hit him over the back of the head.

"Hey, hey, wake up." She gave him a shake, covering her mouth with her free hand to stop the smoke getting in. "Come on, Wren! Get up! We haven't got any time!"

He was slow to open his eyes, but she had no time to wait for him. She started dragging him up, getting him on his feet. "Hey! I don't know if you've noticed this, but your house is on *fire!*"

The fire itself was so loud now that she could barely hear herself think. Ezra had gone quiet. Wren blinked slowly, confused. "What's…?"

"You're going to be fine, okay? Come on, I need your help, or we're never going to get out of here. Work with me now."

As she let go of him, he looked behind her, his eyes going wide. "Look out!"

Hands in her hair. Pain shot through her scalp as she was yanked away from Wren. He grabbed her by the hand, but it slipped from his grasp, his strength nothing compared to who had taken her. Before she could make a sound, before she could react for herself, she was thrown backwards into the fire itself, just as she'd thrown Ezra only moments ago.

It burned, searing into her skin, her nails, her hair. No noise left her throat as she tried to cry out. Elementras with an affinity for fire were only resistant to burns, not immune, and it took everything she had left to even begin shielding herself. Her magic came at her call, more powerful than ever as she desperately tried to protect her body —but it wasn't enough.

She didn't have the strength to save herself from the flames, but she also knew that she couldn't let herself be consumed. Not with Wren still stuck in there, not with Cage Street still burning. Ezra still had to be stopped and she was the only person who could do it.

Nobody else would be the hero. Nobody but her.

It wasn't her power that gave her strength. It was her resolve. She searched in herself for everything she could muster and used it. Bit-by-bit, she fought her way out, the fire around her fighting back as it tried to resist her will. Damn the pain. Damn the consequences. That was what she'd told Cami, and she'd meant it.

Tearing herself free of the fire, she staggered a few steps before dropping to her knees with a scream. It was a guttural sound that sounded splitting even to her own ears. Something had changed within her, rot spreading through her chest, to her limbs. It felt like something had died inside her ribcage, decaying between the bones. It burned even more than the flames that had consumed her, it *raged.*

Her vision cleared in bits and pieces. She choked on the smoke as she forced the pain back, looking up. In the centre of the room, amidst the chaos and the flames, stood Ezra. His already scarce hair had been burned away, his skin scorched beyond repair. He looked like a walking corpse. She wouldn't have recognized him if she hadn't already known it was him.

Wren stared at her, his face twisted half in disgust, half horror.

"Oh, Domi," breathed Ezra. "You look beautiful."

His tone made her nauseous. It would not end unless she ended it herself. Wren covered his mouth to protect himself from the smoke and glanced back towards the doorway, but the way out was blocked off by the fire. He wouldn't survive if this went on any longer.

Burn it down.

Something above them creaked. She looked up, realising that the ceiling was entirely aflame. It would fall in on them, the entire *house* would fall in on them. There was no time.

Burn it down.

As she stood there, Ezra looking at her with those red eyes, Wren backed up to the flames with no way out, she remembered the story of the phoenix. Pain stole most of the memory, but she could still see Caspian on the bed, the pale streaks in his hair standing out against the bland blankets.

"We could do with more hero Ilia," he'd said wistfully.

Burn it down.

The neighbourhood, the house, Ezra—maybe they were all beyond saving. Her own body too. She had nothing left to hold back. Now was not the time to give in.

Now was the time to save what she could.

Her magic didn't need to be called on. It had all but taken over her now, screeching in her ears. With everything she had, she coated herself in her own flames, fashioning herself into the phoenix from the tale. She had no *triash* to boost her power, all she had was her own strength, her own rotting magic. She'd always known that it would kill her eventually, but if that was the case, then she would use it for good.

Burn it down, demanded her magic.

No.

Ezra tried to catch her as she threw herself at him anew, but her flames burned too strong and his strength had waned from being caught in the blaze. "Dominique!" he snapped, his own skin igniting, but she hardly felt him, or anything else anymore. They were on fire together, two Elementra finally swallowed whole in one last stand against one another.

She slammed her fist into his abdomen, tangling their legs

together as they both went down again. Pinning him by his wrists, she let herself burn, catching him in it as she did. They both screamed.

"Dominique!" Ezra rasped. "Let me *go*!"

The ceiling creaked horrifically overhead. She looked up in time to see parts collapse in, scattering heavy debris across the burning room. Wren jumped backwards to dodge it, but the burning chunk between them had pinned him between it and the fire in the hall, all while trapping her in the front room.

As Ezra fought her hold, she called out to Wren in strained tones. "Can you get out?"

"Let him burn!" Ezra hissed. "This is our swan song!"

"No!" She let go of his wrists and grabbed him by the throat. Numbly, she began to squeeze. Any noise he might have made was drowned out by the fire. "This ends here, Ezra. No more!"

He grew more frantic beneath her, but she couldn't let him go. As they pushed against each other, she heard Wren coughing, awful, hacking noises. "Wren! Get out!"

He took a long moment to respond. She couldn't see him behind the debris. "I can't. I can't, there's nothing—!"

He started to cough again. Hopelessness welled up inside her. Had it been for nought? She couldn't move the debris. She couldn't save Wren from fire, or smoke, or heat. If he died in here, then she would have achieved nothing. If he died in here, it would be Ezra's final victory.

Those helpless thoughts weakened her hold on Ezra. He reached up with clawed fingers, his eyes bulging. "This is my domain, Dominique!"

"You know nothing! This isn't—!"

Amidst the flames, amidst the heat, amidst it all, she realised that she felt cool. Her throat hitched as water appeared from nothing, dousing the flames around the debris. She readjusted her grip on Ezra, strengthened by the feeling. Ezra grew weaker beneath her, the life draining out of him, and she had to hang on.

She could win this. She'd have known that icy feeling anywhere. Someone had finally come to help. Someone had given her the break she needed.

"Wren!" Caspian's voice was everything to her in that moment, the relief overwhelming. "Wren, come here, I'll get you out."

"No, you have to wait, Dominique is still there!"

"Domi?" Caspian stumbled over her name. When she looked over, his face appeared in the smouldering gaps in the debris, not quite obscured by the smoke. His eyes went wide as he took in her appearance, all the colour draining from his face.

Ezra knew he was there. With one, burning hand, he weakly reached for her. With the other, he reached towards Caspian. It was such a desperate gesture, and yet she didn't feel a thing for it. He was already dead to her, her heart numb.

She held onto his throat until his limbs went slack, until he stared up at her with glassy, blank eyes, the fire not dying. Slowly, she let go, straightening up and turning her head back towards where Caspian stood behind the debris.

"Get Wren out of here," she said.

Her eyesight was beginning to blur—or was that the smoke? She still made out the way Caspian faltered, how he hesitated even when it mattered the most. "I'm not leaving you!"

"You have to! Get out, now! It's too dangerous to stay!"

"I'm not going!" He began to fight with the debris, but it was futile. He wouldn't be able to move it. "Domi, come on, help me! Don't do this!"

"It's useless." She dissolved the flames from her body and looked up, the house falling apart all around her. Inside, she felt dead already, the pain having faded, the aftershocks no longer coming. Too much of her had already rotted away, just like it had been with Ezra.

"Dominique!"

"Even if I got outside, I wouldn't last long." Dominique closed her eyes so she wouldn't need to see his face. "I've destroyed my body, Caspian. I'm dying, and you know it."

She heard Wren cough again. How much smoke had he inhaled? The sound of rushing water reached her ears, telling her that Caspian was still on his useless crusade. "Domi, you have to let me try. I'm coming, just wait!"

"Don't waste your life on me," she pleaded. "You can still save someone else, so save Wren."

She opened her eyes again in time to see his face fall, agony engraved into his features. "Domi, Domi, I…"

"I love you, Caspy." She had to make him go before it was too late. "I always will, so go."

It was her way of saying goodbye, and judging by his expression, he realised that. After a moment, his face hardened, and finally she saw the bravery in him that she'd always known had existed. They held each other's gaze a moment longer, and as that single second passed them by, she wished once more that she had a different power.

She wanted nothing more than to spend one more day by his side.

He took a deep, shuddery breath. "I love you too, Domi. Wait for me, okay? Please wait. You won't be alone long, I promise."

"Don't be so quick," she replied, offering him a smile. "I don't want to see you so soon."

He stood, and then he was gone, out into the hallway, out of her life. She was alone, only the raging fire and Ezra's corpse for company. It was over.

She was over.

Her energy spent, she let herself collapse beside Ezra. The blaze burned brighter in his death, overhead, at her sides, inside her very core. She'd always known that her life would end in fire. It was the way it went.

She heard the house creak once again, threatening to crumble. This was it. There was no going back.

Closing her eyes, she waited for the end.

CHAPTER 18

EVEN IN THE WAKE OF CASPIAN'S POWER, EZRA'S FLAMES REFUSED TO die down.

Wren waned at his side as they fought to get free of the house, telling Caspian that he had little time before he passed out entirely from the relentless smoke. "Stay awake," Caspian warned him, drawing upon as much of his power as he could to try and put down the flames. The continued to dance in his path, flickering as if he'd never touched them.

The heat came at him from every angle, overpowering, and the weather outside only helped the fire in its destructive path. It was a testament to Ezra's power; even nature bent over backwards to help him, working against everything Caspian was trying to do, fighting back to stop him in his tracks. But he couldn't just give up, not when Dominique had entrusted Wren's life to him. He fought, throwing his power out again, again, pushing back against the heat and the flames, the war not over, the battle not yet decided.

Ezra wouldn't have his victory. Caspian would never let that ending come to pass.

With one more jet of water, a blessed opening presented itself. Dragging Wren through, he did his best to shield both of them from burns, the two of them bursting free of the house and all but collapsing on the burning street. The sun beat down on his back, a relief and a terror all in one.

Caspian's shoulders shook as Wren hacked and coughed, trying to clear his lungs, but it was just as smoky outside. The street itself had filled with people—*Elementras*—just like back in Mellingdale. Once again they'd gathered, trying to fight the fire as one, but it was clear that they weren't enough. It wasn't simply one house, or one row of houses, it was the entire neighbourhood that was burning, and there were so little to their numbers in comparison. Getting to his feet, Caspian made his decision. He had to join them.

"Wren!" Rian's voice made him pause. He turned to see him come hurtling towards them, dropping to his knees and throwing his arms around Wren. "Oh, shit! Are you alright? Answer me, Wren, I thought you were *dead*!"

"He..." Wren's expression was blank when he turned his head to look at the blazing shell that had been his home. There was nothing to it, no shock, no fear, no despair. "He did this, all because I..."

Caspian looked too, hoping that, at any moment, Dominique might emerge from the fire. He couldn't wipe the image of her from his mind, how she'd looked like that bird she'd crafted from flame. She'd had blazing wings as she'd knelt over Ezra, her eyes gleaming like the fire, her hair all burnt away and her face twisted in agony.

Come back to me, he begged silently. *Please, just come back. I need you.*

The house answered him with a low rumble. The seconds slowed as the roof of Wren's family home collapsed in on itself, and Caspian could only watch in silence as the fire swallowed everything that was left in its unrelenting fury.

It refused to stop, even in the face of his grief. It welled up inside him, his magic weeping in his ears.

Wash it away, it said. *Wash it away. Wash it away. Wash it away!*

"Caspian?" Rian said, still holding onto Wren like his life depended on it, the horror in his eyes undeniable. "Don't tell me, was Dominique still in there?"

Caspian had no response for him. Instead, he left them there to join the other Elementras. There was nothing else he could do now for Dominique except this. He never had been able to turn away from people in need, and who else needed him more than the Elementras who were fighting so hard to quell the flames?

Using the power of the other Elementras around him, he drew his water up into his hands, focusing it skyward. Like before, the water gathered in a whirlpool-like structure, growing wider, wider. He held onto it, letting it build, letting the other Elementra contribute.

Wash it away, his magic demanded.

He did. He gave it everything he had, more power than he'd ever used in one expulsion, all powered by his own sorrow. He stood there, watching as it began to pour down over Cage Street, every Elementra around him adding to it, bolstering his efforts, feeding into his despair.

The hottest day of the year, everything working against him, his magic already exhausted from his work, and Caspian Fay was making it rain.

"Caspian." Rian's voice came behind him. When he looked over his shoulder, he found him there with Wren, helping him stand. "What are you doing?"

Caspian felt water on his cheeks. His own tears. Dominique was gone. Ezra too, but it was no comfort. Everything he'd ever known had been ripped out from under him in seconds. He'd lost it all.

"I'm putting this place out, no matter what it takes," he said.

His physical energy left him. He dropped his knees, still watching as the downpour he'd fuelled came crashing down. Still, he gave more of himself to it, working against the weather for the outcome he desired. The surrounding area cooled, his power spilling out of him uncontrolled. Other Elementra turned to look at him, awestruck.

"Caspian," Wren said. "Just stop."

Not until it was over. When the aftershocks began to hit, he barely realised that it was his own body fighting back. It was nothing compared to the pain of losing her. Even as he screamed, the rain did not falter.

He would stay until the fire was dead.

～

The next morning, the papers were awash with the same headlines that would come to adorn the front pages for the weeks to come. Despite Caspian's best efforts, the Cage Street Inferno took the lives of eighteen people, including Isaac and Olivia Sharp who had been dining at a friend's home only two doors down at the time. The number didn't include Ezra, but did include Dominique. An unnamed Ilpolitia officer gave a statement on her behalf, claiming that the force itself had failed her, and that more should have been done to prevent such an outcome.

None of it mattered to Caspian. That day, he wandered the city of Aquiline in a daze, looking for a purpose, for some reason to carry on. He hadn't seen Wren or Rian since the Ilpol had arrived in Nadre-end, and he had no intention of searching for them either. They had enough baggage to deal with, just as he had his.

In the end, as the sun rose on the second morning after Dominique's death, Caspian had no choice but to return to the inn. He hadn't slept since the fire despite all the energy he'd used, hadn't been able to with the memories haunting him every time he closed his eyes. He wondered if he'd ever be able to rest again.

Aquiline itself felt like it had stopped around him as it tried to recover. The papers had no idea what Ezra's motive was, and Caspian would never know either, closure forever out of reach. All anyone knew was that an Ilia had killed multiple officers of the Ilpolitia before going on to burn down an entire street, and in turn, the papers called it anarchism, a demonstration on how badly Ilia were treated.

It wasn't the truth. Caspian called it an addiction, one that had gone too far, but it didn't matter now. The city would crack down on all Ilia, and the sanctions on them would only get harsher. The papers hadn't made a single mention of all the Ilia who had rushed to help when things had gotten bad, they'd only focused on the actions of one man who had torn a wealthy street apart.

When Caspian finally got back to the inn, the room was still in the state they'd left it in. The blankets were pushed back where he and Dominique had laid as she'd told him the story of the phoenix. He fell onto the pillows and thought of her with those blazing wings. A sob worked its way up his throat, and he didn't have it in him to fight it any longer.

He cried until sleep finally dragged it away from him. His dreams were scorched in flames, and when he awoke next, the sun was setting. Sitting up, he stared at his shaking hands and wondered what he could even do next.

Without Dominique by his side, nothing felt right. He'd become weaker, drained and faded, the emptiest he'd ever been. When he stood and caught sight of himself in the dirty mirror opposite the bed, he realised why. His eyes were bluer than ever, swirls of magic still caught in his irises despite the fact that he hadn't drawn upon any in two days. His hair had lost more colour in the roots, paler than before.

Working with the blacksmith and fighting the fire in Cage Street had done something irreversible to him. His magic showed on him now more than ever. He sat in front of the mirror, reaching out to touch the glass. It was heart-breaking to realise just how little he recognized the person staring back.

Who was he, after everything? Not the same Caspian he'd been before it all, that was certain. Laying back on the floor, he imagined Dominique laying on the bed above him, just like she might have been any time before.

"How did it feel to be the hero?" he asked her.

Silence answered him. Of course, he wasn't insane, he didn't expect a reply. Still, he imagined one all the same. He knew what she'd say.

"I didn't do anything. All those people still died. The entire neighbourhood still burned."

"You did do something, though," Caspian said softly. "If you hadn't taken him down, I don't think Cage Street would have been the end. You saved us all from him, Domi. You did that, all on your own."

Wherever she was, he hoped she heard.

On the third day after her death, he finally went home. Now that

Ezra was gone, there was nothing left to stop him. The door was still stuck from where he'd jammed it shut, but a little bit of jiggling got it to swing open. The hall leading in felt alien, lit in the wrong kind of light. The last time he'd walked in here, Dominique had been going to work, and he'd had no idea what awaited him. It had been normal. It had been calm.

Their bedroom still smelled faintly of her, of the perfumes she liked to wear. Old, worn makeup still sat on the side, touches of her that remained in the house, each one more painful than the last. He wouldn't be able to stay there, not with the cost, but he still had what was left of their savings. Maybe he could find somewhere new with what remained.

Before he left, he filled up a bag with the most important of belongings (the bottles of perfumes, a packet of her matchsticks, the clothes he'd need) and then took one last look around their room. A book he'd forgotten about remained on the table by her bed, one he vaguely recognized. She'd been reading it before they'd needed to leave.

It was a thick tome with no title, borrowed from a library in Ardrend. Dominique had left a bookmark inside, and when he turned to the page it marked, he found a stunning illustration. A phoenix the size of a human being stood before a man, its wings outstretched, the man staring on in awe. The entire image was swathed in gold, the colour not at all faded. The phoenix itself blazed.

"*Dance of Flames*," Caspian said, reading the title of the story aloud. He tried to smile, but his face crumpled. "I see."

He clutched the book close. He would return it to the library, the bookmark left inside. Whoever came across it next, he could only hope that they would be as inspired by the stories as Dominique had been.

∾

Later, after he'd dropped everything off at the inn and returned the book, Caspian went to The Otherground.

It was mid-afternoon and nearly empty. Cami instantly set a drink in front of him when he sat down, not even giving him time to say hello. Instead, she cut in ahead, sombrely telling him, "I heard the news."

Caspian stared at the drink. Alcohol had never really been his thing. "Which parts?"

"What was in the papers, but I'm not stupid enough to believe that it was the full story." She sighed, shaking her head. "It's a shame. I really liked her."

Caspian hummed a non-committal response. Picking up the glass, he peered into the liquid, putting it down when he caught a glimpse of his reflection. His stomach flipped at the thought of drinking it, and even more at the thought of food. He'd had no appetite at all the past few days.

"How are you doing, Caspian?" Cami asked, not moving from her spot in front of him. "The papers are all about the dead, but it's those who lived who have to deal with the aftermath. So, are you okay?"

He laid his head down on the counter, resting on his arms. "I'm the best I can be."

"Brave answer."

"It's the answer she'd like."

"I reckon you're right about that." When he glanced up at her, she offered him a small smile. "You seem different, like there's a little more to you. First time I met you, I thought that you might blow away if the wind pushed you too hard. Now I get the feeling you might push back."

"Really?" Caspian thought about his reflection and understood what she meant. "Thank you. I'm just thinking about all of it, and…I'm glad. Glad that I got to say goodbye. If I'd been any later, I wouldn't have gotten that. But then I think that and I start wondering, if I'd been earlier, maybe I could have done something different."

Cami drummed her fingers on the counter. "Do you really think you could have changed what happened?"

Caspian thought it through. Dominique had said she was dying, that even if she'd gotten out, she wouldn't have made it. Her magic had ruined her the way it was ruining him. He knew that as fact.

140

"I wish I could have," he said, "but I think she knew she was at the end. That's why she went all out."

One day, in the near future, he might be faced with the same dilemma. He'd seen the evidence in the mirror. He could only hope that, when the time came, he would face his fate with the same courage that Dominique had.

Though death still terrified him, the thought that she was waiting for him blunted the edges of his fear.

"You're a lot stronger than I gave you credit for," Cami said, taking his drink to sip for herself. "So, Caspian Fay, now that it's over, what will you do now? It's the first day of summer today, did you know? It's as good a time as any to start anew."

Leaving Aquiline was out of the question now, and it wasn't like there was anything left to run away *from*. Sitting back up, Caspian said, "I'm going to make the most out of the time I have left. I know it's limited, I've known for a while, but seeing what happened with Dominique and Ezra has made it real for me. I'm not going to last forever."

Cami blinked, looking a little taken aback. "That's…"

Caspian forced a smile to his face. "I'll be okay. Maybe not right now, but I will be."

He took the rest of the drink and drank it in one. It burned a path down his throat, and maybe, just maybe, it was what he needed after all. "To you, Domi. I'll see you soon."

Behind him, he heard the doors creak. Cami stilled in response, her hand flying up to her face, but she said nothing.

"What is it?" Caspian asked, turning on his stall to look. What he saw surprised him. Wren and Rian stood at the entrance, but there was an air about them telling Caspian that, just as he was not the same Caspian who had existed before the fire, these were not the same boys he'd met on that smoky night all those weeks ago. Wren had the hood of his jacket drawn up, his face hidden by the shadows it cast, and Rian had his hands in his pockets, his shoulders shaking almost imperceptibly.

"Well, look who it is!" Rian said, overly bright. He crossed the bar and took his usual seat, Wren following behind. "Been a bit of a while, Caspian. You're looking well."

You're not, Caspian thought. When Rian asked for a drink, Caspian noticed that his hands were shaking too. His face was drawn, dark shadows under his eyes like he hadn't slept in days. He didn't look right, not the fun-loving young man from before, but someone entirely different.

"Where have you been?" he asked, looking between Wren and Rian. "You both went missing after everything, and I thought…I didn't know if I'd ever see you again."

Rian laughed, tipping his head back as if Caspian had told a joke. "Where have we been indeed? Nowhere. Not that it's any of your business."

How many times had Rian told him that now? He was a far cry from the open man he'd known before. In the wake of his father's death, he'd become cagier, harder to engage.

"Since when have you been so secretive?" Wren asked, dropping his hood to finally show his face. Caspian froze in place, both him and Cami staring in stunned silence.

A ghastly, ragged-looking scar marred the right side of his face. It looked as if it had been a deep wound once, cutting down from above his eye and finishing by his lip. It disfigured his face, his boyish looks torn through.

He hadn't been wounded in the fire, not like that. From an open wound to a scar like that in less than three days? It was impossible.

"What happened to you?" Caspian blurted out, unable to stop himself.

"No," Cami said. "What did you *do?*"

Wren and Rian both looked at one another before they both burst out laughing. When the light hit them just right, Caspian swore that he saw magic in their eyes, bright green, just like the blue he'd seen in his own, in the red he'd seen in Dominique's, in Ezra. It wasn't Elementra magic. It wasn't Empathra either, which shone purple. This was something different, something Caspian hadn't ever seen on anyone in Aquiline before.

There was only one way for normal folk to access Ilia magic, and that was to travel to a split and make a deal with it. Cami hadn't noticed, but Caspian had.

"You didn't," he said, breathless. "Tell me that you didn't."

"We had an adventure," Wren said, his eyes just a touch brighter than usual, unnoticeable to someone who wouldn't be looking for it. "There's nothing wrong with that now, is there?"

AFTERWORD

This is actually the second edition of this book! To reflect that, I'm writing a second afterword, but I'll leave the original intact for you to read below.

I wrote the original *Dance of Flames* in 2018, which feels like a lifetime ago. The original version was my first venture into long form, and while it was okay, I was never fully comfortable with it. Being the debut for both myself and the Ilia Chronicles, I wanted it to fully showcase my abilities, and so here it is once more. Not much has changed, the general storyline remained the same, but I made some slight adjustments to the minor details. I hope Caspian and Dominique feel more rounded with these changes, and that their relationship feels more organic!

Skills change, and I feel like my writing style from 2018 was a bit of a different beast to what it is now. The world of Ilia has been expanded greatly since I wrote this story, heading into another continent and unfurling extra lore, so there's plenty more to come. As of writing this, the fourth book in the Ilia Chronicles series (*In Starlight's Wake*) is finished, and just currently going through beta reads. I hope you'll look forward to it.

I think that's everything? The story should read far smoother nowadays, which puts my weary heart at ease haha. It's been nice to revisit Dominique and Caspian. Perhaps I'll have a look into *The Eternal Garden* next…

(14/12/2018 , Original Afterword)

This is rather surreal, to realise that I'm sitting here writing the final note on this tiny book. It's been a complicated two-year long relationship with this story, and in an interesting turn of events, it actually ended up being my debut. Caspian's story has come to a close for now, while Wren and Rian have a lot still ahead of them. I hope you'll enjoy their next outing.

So, with that, onto my other thank you notes! First, to my parents for constantly discussing their novel ideas when I was just a teeny tiny baby listening in on things I didn't really understand. I don't think I'd be here without that influence.

Secondly, onto my sisters. Alexa, you helped shape Wren's personality more than you probably realise. Shayla, you listened to me rabbit on about every element of this story when it was still just a skeleton. You guys are the best.

To my friends who stood by me for the entire journey, and especially Caroline, who provided me writerly-advice and listened to my ranting and raging when elements of this story proved difficult, and Lauren, who encouraged me all the time. You're stars.

And finally, to you, who saw this book and decided that you might like the story in its pages. Writing is a lonely craft, but to finally be able to share the prologue to Wren and Rian's story means the world to me. Until we meet again!

ALSO BY JORDANNA JADE

THE ILIA CHRONICLES:

Dance of Flames (1)

The Eternal Garden (2)

Choosing Divinity (3)

In Starlight's Wake (4)

SHADONIUS:

Shadows in the Night (1)

Printed in Great Britain
by Amazon

73842775R00092